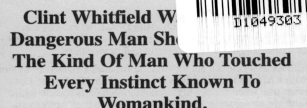

Clint Whitfield W... Dangerous Man Sh... The Kind Of Man Who Touched Every Instinct Known To Womankind.

Although she enjoyed the sensual art of flirtation, she'd become wary of deeper involvement. So she'd decided she didn't need romance in her life. Friendship would do.

But this man had stirred something deep inside her, something innocent of prior experience. And he'd done it without the usual social exchanges, with little verbal or physical communication, and without using an ounce of masculine charm.

Baffled by his effect on her, Regina studied the sculpted features now softened by slumber, the challenging, provocative scar. "Yep, dangerous," she murmured, a smile touching her mouth. "Wonderfully dangerous."

Dear Reader,

Welcome to the world of Silhouette Desire, where you can indulge yourself every month with romances that can only be described as passionate, powerful and provocative!

Silhouette's beloved author Annette Broadrick returns to Desire with a MAN OF THE MONTH who is *Hard To Forget*. Love rings true when former high school sweethearts reunite while both are on separate undercover missions to their hometown. Bestselling writer Cait London offers you *A Loving Man,* when a big-city businessman meets a country girl and learns the true meaning of love.

The Desire theme promotion THE BABY BANK, about sperm-bank client heroines who find love unexpectedly, returns with Amy J. Fetzer's *Having His Child*, part of her WIFE, INC. miniseries. The tantalizing Desire miniseries THE FORTUNES OF TEXAS: THE LOST HEIRS continues with *Baby of Fortune* by Shirley Rogers. In *Undercover Sultan*, the second book of Alexandra Sellers's SONS OF THE DESERT: THE SULTANS trilogy, a handsome prince is forced to go on the run with a sexy mystery woman—who may be the enemy. And Ashley Summers writes of a Texas tycoon who comes home to find a beautiful stranger living in his mansion in *Beauty in His Bedroom*.

This month see inside for details about our exciting new contest "Silhouette Makes You a Star." You'll feel like a star when you delve into all six fantasies created in Desire books this August!

Enjoy!

Joan Marlow Golan

Joan Marlow Golan
Senior Editor, Silhouette Desire

Please address questions and book requests to:
Silhouette Reader Service
U.S.: 3010 Walden Ave., P.O. Box 1325, Buffalo, NY 14269
Canadian: P.O. Box 609, Fort Erie, Ont. L2A 5X3

Beauty in
His Bedroom
ASHLEY SUMMERS

Published by Silhouette Books
America's Publisher of Contemporary Romance

To Rita Gallagher,
mentor, companion and best friend.
Thank you for being in my life.

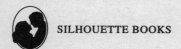 SILHOUETTE BOOKS

ISBN 0-373-76386-7

BEAUTY IN HIS BEDROOM

Copyright © 2001 by Faye Ashley

Books by Ashley Summers

Silhouette Desire

Fires of Memory #36
The Marrying Kind #95
Juliet #291
Heart's Delight #374
Eternally Eve #509
Heart's Ease #675
On Wings of Love #1050
That Loving Touch #1257
Beauty in His Bedroom #1386

Silhouette Romance

Season of Enchantment #197
A Private Eden #223

ASHLEY SUMMERS

is an incurable romantic who lives in Texas, in a house that overflows with family and friends. Her busy life revolves around the man she married thirty years ago, her three children and her handsome grandson, Eric. Formerly the owner and operator of a landscaping firm, she also enjoys biking, aerobics, reading and traveling.

SILHOUETTE MAKES YOU A STAR!
Feel like a star with Silhouette.
Look for the exciting details of our new contest
inside all of these fabulous Silhouette novels:

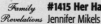

One

Regina Flynn stepped into the elegant, two-story foyer with a wariness bordering on the absurd. As an employee of Lamar's Home Maintenance and Security Agency, she had a perfect right to enter this uninhabited home. Yet the sound of her heels on the black-and-white marble floor was shockingly loud, and her heart beat so fast she felt dizzy.

Regina stopped just inside the door, her little blue pot of African violets clutched to her chest like a talisman. Even the August heat did not warm her inner chill. Closing the door, she leaned against its hard surface with a gusty sigh.

"I've done it," she whispered. "I've stolen a house."

A sharp shake of head immediately rejected this preposterous notion; the assistant to Lamar's regional manager did not steal houses! Her position with the agency placed her in charge of the North Houston area, and this handsome estate, owned by a man named Clint Whitfield, was merely part of her portfolio of managed properties.

"All you've *done* is assign him a house sitter, Regina," she corrected herself crisply. "You do have that authority, you know. The house sitter just happens to be you."

Annoyed with herself—and an overly active conscience she could never quite master—Regina felt for the light switch. In the growing dusk, the boxes holding her belongings looked pitifully few; when a chandelier flooded the area with light, they appeared even more misplaced.

Sadness tightened her throat. Everything she owned fit easily into six cardboard boxes. Not much of a legacy for twenty-nine years of living, she thought dispiritedly.

Catching sight of herself in an ornate wall mirror, Regina pushed at the red-gold curls swirling around her face in riotous disarray. "Flynn, you're a mess," she snapped at her green-eyed image. Her voice seemed to rebound off the walls.

Edging around boxes, she walked down the hall. White-shrouded furniture haunted darkened rooms. Chilled air blew through concealed vents, a necessity in Houston's humid climate despite the absence of people. Air-conditioning, not ghosts, caused her goose bumps, she chided her quick shiver.

She paused in the sculptural arch of another doorway. Beyond lay the great room, a huge, airy space that encompassed the kitchen, breakfast nook and dining room wing, the family room, and glass-roofed conservatory forming the rear wall. She felt a little foolish bringing this modest violet into such opulence. With exaggerated care she centered it on the kitchen windowsill. Almost magically it meshed with its setting.

"As if to the manor born," she quipped, patting a velvety leaf. "You're just what this house needed."

Flipping another light switch, she caught her breath at the beauty its mellow glow revealed. Clint Whitfield had built something really special, she thought softly.

So why had he left it vacant for so long?

As usual, her thorny question went unanswered. She didn't know Clint Whitfield; she'd been in another department when he contracted with the agency. Later, a promotion had put her in charge of his file, and she'd been inside his gracious, white-columned abode several times on routine inspections of the lawn-and-maid services included in his contract.

As months stretched into years, she strongly disagreed with his decision to leave it empty while he was out of the country. But she kept her opinions to herself and did not overstep her authority.

Until the fire.

Regina tensed as painful memories deluged her heart. She no longer had a home. In June, a fire had destroyed her frame dwelling and all its contents. The only silver lining was that her adored young sister had been spared the ordeal; Katie, fifteen, was away at her special school.

Still, it had been a heart-wrenching experience. Although mentally handicapped, Katie's emotions were unimpaired, and when told of the loss of her childhood home, she'd cried like the devastated child she was. Regina cried with her. Then, resolute, she began putting her life back together.

Despite her good salary, she found it tough; Katie's

school was very expensive. Regina had rented a cheap kitchenette apartment and hated it. *And there sat Clint Whitfield's beautiful, fully furnished house going to waste while he roamed Africa.*

Regina sighed. Before the fire, such indifference had been an irritant. Afterwards, it had outraged her. To own such a treasure and not care about it!

She'd made allowances for him. Then he'd renewed his contract for yet another year. After brief but intense thought, Regina made a decision; given his continuing absence he needed a house sitter. Volunteering herself for the task would resolve both their problems.

As required, she'd fired off a letter to him stating her intent, but after two weeks he still hadn't answered, which wasn't unusual; except for that prompt, annual check for services rendered there'd been little correspondence from him. *So you shrugged off your doubts and just moved in,* Regina ended wryly.

Musingly she studied her new abode. Although beautifully furnished, there was no art on the walls, no family pictures. Strange. Why no personal items? She didn't know much about the man beyond his vital statistics. She hadn't checked him out—why should she? To her he was just another rich guy who considered beautiful houses as interchangeable as bedsheets.

Beautiful women, too, most likely, she thought tartly. She knew he was unmarried because he'd checked that box on his application form.

Regina shrugged. She didn't give a hoot about her client's marital status, or his character, either, for that matter. She only cared about his schedule. Renewing his contract meant Clint Whitfield wouldn't be home for another year.

Relaxing for the first time since she'd entered his

house, Regina pulled the pins from her hair and ran her fingers through the curly, shoulder-length mane. She was through worrying about her actions. When he would notify the agency of his expected return, she'd be out of the house in a flash. Until then, she was...

"Home," Regina whispered with a trace of defiance, then raised her voice assertively. "I'm home."

It was half past six on a fine September day when Clint Whitfield came home again. An unsettling impulse, he acknowledged, but hell, he was only in town for one night; common sense dictated that he sleep in his own bed rather than in a hotel.

Entering the circular driveway, Clint parked in front of the house, but made no move to get out. Houston was having one of its rare, exquisitely tender sunsets and the velvety lawn was awash with golden light.

Its loveliness hurt rather than pleased. His broad shoulders stiffened; tension flowed down his taut body. This used to be his favorite time of day. He hated it now. Hated September, for that matter. He'd lost the only thing worth living for on one dark September night.

For a moment longer Clint sat in his car, his gaze fixed on the manor-style dwelling silhouetted against the vast Texas sky. *The house he had built for his beloved.*

His stomach knotted at all there was to face here. Anger thinned his mouth—dammit, coming home shouldn't be this difficult! It had been nearly three years since he'd left. *Ran,* he amended with a twisted smile. But you couldn't run fast enough or far enough to outrace memory. The nightmarish image prowling the edges of his mind like some caged beast was proof of that.

Clint's blue eyes narrowed as he gazed at the rose bed to the right of the house. Barbara's roses. They almost flaunted their vibrant blooms. He felt a gust of outrage that they had outlived the woman who planted them.

Of course she hadn't done the actual planting; those delicate hands couldn't risk physical labor. His wife had been a skilled pediatric surgeon. Someone the world needed, he thought bleakly. He was a veterinarian. But she had died and he still lived, and of what real use to the world was one vet more or less?

Clint's caustic question reflected his inner landscape like a mirror. Wearily he maneuvered his six-foot-plus frame out of the rental car. "This damn thing!" he muttered, pulling himself erect. He needed his old pickup truck, big and roomy enough for a man to sit comfortably, he thought, slamming the door.

An instant later he opened it again, and reached across the seat for his treasured Stetson. The battered hat, once tan, now faded to a soft cream by fierce jungle suns, had traveled the world with him. He set it on his dark head and angled the brim, a gesture of bravado, for the strong legs that had carried him around for thirty-five years felt ridiculously unsteady.

Clint closed the door with unnecessary force. Why the hell had he come back? There was nothing here for him. Certainly not this blasted house—he didn't care if he ever saw it again. Tight-mouthed, he strode up the wide brick walk, his decision solidifying as he mounted the steps. Sell the place. Get rid of everything. Be free of it. He didn't expect to ever feel happy again, but maybe he could at least find peace of mind.

His footsteps echoed in the still air. The house would echo, too, he thought, unlocking the door. Doubtless it would be as well kept as the grounds, thanks to the maintenance agency. But he dreaded stepping inside those empty, musty rooms.

They'd be filled with shrouded furniture, of course. But the house would still be empty. As empty as his heart, he reflected without a trace of pathos. Opening the door, he walked into the foyer and stopped dead.

For a moment Clint thought his heart would stop, too. He had a blurred image of fresh flowers and handsome plants where none should be, for he'd told no one of his homecoming. But what stunned him were the aromas wafting on the cool, decidedly unmusty air. Someone was cooking!

Italian, he thought, sniffing. Spicy, tomatoey, garlicky—the kind of food he loved. The sense of déjà vu was overwhelming. For the briefest instant he slipped from the present into the past, when just such delicious odors welcomed him home from work.

A sound from the kitchen jolted him back to reality. *There was no one to welcome him home from work— there never would be again.* Giving himself a savage shake, he took off his hat, then stood there crushing the brim in his fingers. He wasn't imagining things— someone really *was* cooking!

His eyes slitted; anger ticked a muscle in his jaw. Was this somebody's idea of a joke? Treading quietly on the gleaming wood floor, he entered the great room.

Surprise stopped him again. Plants filled the sweeping curve of tall, Palladian windows. In the den, a lamp burned beside his leather chair, and a book lay facedown on the cushion. Pink satin house slippers lay nearby, as if lazily kicked off.

"What the *hell!*" he muttered, mauling his hair.

Depositing his hat on the built-in desk, he looked around for the source of sound he'd heard. Only a half wall separated the kitchen proper from the breakfast nook, and at first he thought it empty. Then a young woman emerged from the pantry carrying a pewter bowl.

Clint experienced a swirl of vivid impressions. She wore jeans, a pink T-shirt and big, round glasses with purple frames. Her face was a valentine, her nose, small and sassy. Unpolished nails tipped her bare feet, and a bouquet of red-gold curls bloomed wildly atop her head. He hadn't the faintest idea who she was.

That topknot of hair swayed precariously as she caught sight of him. Eyes as green as springtime flew wide behind those absurd glasses. She screamed and dropped the bowl, which hit the tiled floor with a resounding clang.

"It's all right. I won't hurt you!" Clint said. Hoping to prevent another outburst, he flung out his hands reassuringly.

She backed against the counter, her eyes enormous.

His heart contracted. "Please, don't be scared. I'm Clint Whitfield. I own this house." He stepped closer. "I'm sorry. I really didn't mean to scare you. I just let myself in and then I heard..." His eyebrows shot together as the situation hit home. "Wait a minute—who are you, anyway? And what are you doing in my house?"

"R-Regina. Regina Flynn. Gina." Collecting herself, she pressed a hand to her throat. "My goodness!" she exclaimed with a tremulous laugh. "You'll have to forgive me, Mr. Whitfield. Obviously you caught me by surprise."

"Obviously."

"Uh, yes. And I'm here because…" She bent down to pick up the bowl, and with precise movements, placed it on the counter.

Stalling, he thought, eyes narrowing again as she straightened. "Because?" he prompted.

Her eyes flinted and that pointed chin came up. Deliberately she removed her glasses. "Because I'm supposed to be here. I'm with the Lamar Home Maintenance Agency, and among other things I'm a house sitter. House-sitting your house," she added. "It's just part of the agency's service." Her gaze collided with his. "Wait a minute—you're not supposed to be here. You didn't notify me that you were returning!"

"I didn't know I had to notify you that I was returning," Clint replied with cutting sarcasm. Twice in as many minutes, he'd literally had the wind knocked out of him. "And I don't recall asking the *agency*," he mocked, "for this particular service."

"Well, then your recall is wrong," she retorted with a little more spirit.

"Is it now! I don't think so, lady." Clint's nostrils flared as a wisp of fragrant steam rose from the kettle simmering on the stove. His kettle, his stove. It was spaghetti sauce. His irritation swelled into a roar that he swatted down with sheer willpower. Be damned if he was going to lose his temper!

"No," he continued, his voice soft and steely. "I think what's wrong is your presence on my property. In fact, I doubt you're even with the agency, I think you just found an empty house, moved in and made yourself at home. Maybe even sold off a few things when you needed pocket money," he added, looking around. Nothing appeared to be missing, but then he'd been gone so long, who remembered? "Maybe I should call the police."

"The police! But that's crazy, I'm not a thief—there isn't a thing missing from your house!" she replied, her bosom heaving with indignation.

It really did heave, Clint thought, startled at his interest. The T-shirt displayed her small breasts to perfection. His willful gaze traveled down her slim waist to the soft denim hugging her thighs and long legs. She was tall for a woman—five foot nine, he estimated. And although trim and fit, she was no clothes-horse. She had hips, thighs and buttocks, he noted in that fleeting but quite intense scrutiny.

When he brought his gaze back to her face, she squared her shoulders and firmed up her mouth.

"If you'll stop making these asinine accusations and let me explain, I'm sure we can clear this up," she said. "I am with the agency and I am your house sitter—not some *squatter* staking a claim on your property!" she added with emerald-eyed disdain. "Personally I think you're very fortunate to have me here looking after your interests. I've taken very good care of your home, Mr. Whitfield, really, I have."

She waved a slim, rose-tipped hand, encompassing the immaculate kitchen and den. "You can see that for yourself if you'll just look around. But now that you're back," she said hastily, "I'll be quick to pack up my stuff and leave without further ado. I'll tell the agency that you're back—you needn't bother yourself, I'll be glad to do it for you."

She gave him a piercingly sweet smile.

Clint's head suddenly reeled. He stepped back from her. "I bet you will," he drawled, his annoyance almost too hot to handle. "But why don't I just tell them myself?" He reached for the telephone.

"You go right ahead and do that!" she snapped, then bit her lip. "Except it would do you no good. In the end you'd only get me. I mean, I'm in charge of you. Your file, that is." Her head lowered a fraction, but she still met his gaze. "It says in your contract that you did want this service."

He leaned against the counter, studying her. He didn't *want* to listen to her, he wanted to—needed to— vent this unreasoning anger. Besides, she was nervous about something. Not exactly lying—with those eyes, how could she lie? They had such depth and clarity. Moss green now, with little gold specks, tiny islands in a dusky sea that threatened to engulf him.

Startled anew, Clint jerked his gaze away. "Now why would my contract say a thing like that? I certainly don't remember putting it in there. In fact, when I left here I didn't give a damn about this house. I handed it over to Lamar's because it was the practical thing to do. And God knows I've always been practical," he said with gritty irony. "Protect your investment, Whitfield, I told myself."

Clint shook his head. "Some bloody investment," he added, looking around the lovely room. God, the bitter fights over this fine, Italian-tile floor and hand-carved cabinetry, those soaring windows... Catching himself in an iron grip, he shut down the sudden flow of memory. "Well?" he prodded, glaring at the aggravating Flynn woman. "What do you have to say for yourself?"

His forceful demand seemed to fire rather than quell her defiance. Her eyes flashed. She threw back her head and that chin came up like an arrow aimed straight for his Adam's apple.

"I'll tell you what I have to say! People like you make me sick, Clint Whitfield!"

Clint reared back. "People like *me?*"

"Yes, people like you! You have the money to build beautiful homes like this one, surround yourself with fine furniture, a fancy swimming pool and a big backyard, all the lovely things other people can only dream of. And then you walk off and leave it sitting empty! For *years,* Mr. Whitfield, just sitting here, lonely and devoid of life, not even a skeletal staff to tend it. You just abandoned it!" she accused with a passion that quite astonished Clint.

"Abandoned?" he echoed, his own anger rising to match the blaze in those green eyes. "This house was hardly abandoned, Miss Flynn!"

"All right, I concede that—but it *felt* abandoned!" She snatched a breath. "And don't give me that look!" she warned fiercely. "It's a *home,* Mr. Whitfield, and homes can feel abandoned just like people can! But you don't care, do you? Like you said, you don't give a damn for this house—it means nothing to you. You just take off on a some selfish whim and leave it behind like a cast-off garment!"

She stepped closer, a stiff finger poking his chest for emphasis. "You're a careless man, Mr. Whitfield, and there's nothing worse in my opinion."

Furiously confused, Clint removed himself from her punishing finger. "I couldn't care less about your opinion, Miss Flynn," he roared with his own quite astonishing passion. "But I can get you *fired,* lady! So you'd damn well better care about mine!"

Wheeling, he strode through the room and slammed out the front door.

Regina Flynn stayed frozen to the spot, the fury of his exit still ringing in her ears. "Dear God, what have I done?" she whispered. She flung her hands to her cheeks. "Lost your temper, speared him with a fingernail, called him names, that's all! You idiot!" she berated her fiery loss of control.

Breathing in and out, something she actually had to think about in order to do it correctly, she found her way to the couch. Her knees were weak, her insides quivering. From what, the threat he'd implied? Or the immediate and powerful attraction he had exerted on her flurried senses?

Closing her eyes, Regina pictured his face, hard, dangerous, tough as leather—he'd scared the wits out of her at first! Until that quick, sudden smile. It had touched something within her, a chord that had never been played before...

A grin etched her mouth. There was something strangely wonderful about being near Clint Whitfield. Even when he was roaring at her. Lord, she marveled, who would have guessed he'd be so attractive?

"Stop thinking below the waist, Flynn. He really could cause trouble. That's the important thing here—*I can get you fired, lady*." She mimicked his voice.

And he just might. Chilled, Regina hugged a pillow to her chest. Indignation still sputtered inside her—she hadn't done anything wrong! Not really. "It's not my fault if he doesn't bother reading his mail," she fumed, mangling the pillow.

Tears wet her cheeks. An emotional woman, she cried easily. Too easily. *I shouldn't have blown up like that. I should have explained, tried reasoning with him. Softly, sensibly. Instead I yelled like a fishwife. He's probably on his way to the agency right now, boiling mad, demanding my head. Or job.*

Was he the kind of man who'd do a thing like that?

Regina chewed her lip as she pondered her question. "But I didn't *do* anything! He needed house-sitter services and I provided them," she hissed into the accusing silence.

Nothing wrong with that, she continued her self-argument; hadn't she made other decisions on his behalf with just a follow-up letter? He hadn't responded to her message, but he *had* been duly informed. Or so she told herself when conscience pricked pinholes in logic. Like now.

Drying her eyes, Regina got up and went to stir her spaghetti sauce before it, too, was ruined. Okay, so maybe she had overstepped a bit, she conceded, nibbling her lip. But it had seemed so sensible and harmless at the time! Who could have guessed he'd come home without telling anyone?

And who could have guessed he'd have blue, blue eyes framed by thick, dusky lashes? And a scar—wasn't there a scar on his face? And his voice, so deep. His callused hands and long, hard fingers...

Blankly Regina stared at the wooden spoon in her hand, too distracted to remember what she meant to do with it. Shaking off her beguiled trance, she stirred the contents of the pot, round and round. Granted, her irate client didn't have much of a case, but he could sure raise some dust. Sighing, she turned off the fire under her sauce. She wasn't hungry. The prospect of being fired played havoc with a person's appetite.

"Oh, nonsense, Flynn, you're not going to be fired," she scoffed. Clint Whitfield might have a temper, but he wouldn't carry things *that* far.

Would he?

Two

Several miles away, Clint Whitfield sat at a stoplight, wrapped in baffled wonder. What was wrong with him? He couldn't think straight—he couldn't even see straight. For an instant the newly risen moon seemed to dance in its nest of fleecy clouds. He hadn't even noticed that night had fallen. Apparently he'd been driving aimlessly and for quite a while.

He rubbed his eyes and blew out a long breath. He was just tired, that's all. Bone tired. He'd been traveling for the better part of two days now, in and out of airports, on and off planes. "And still haven't arrived at a destination," he muttered, his irritation ballooning as he remembered he still had to find somewhere to sleep tonight.

At least he knew where the bafflement stemmed from. That Flynn woman. His run-in with her certainly hadn't eased his fatigue. What the hell was he going to do about her?

A silly question. "Kick her out, of course," he answered. "You know damn good and well she's in your house illegally. Without your authorization, anyway," he amended, adverse to using such a strong word. Maybe she really had told him about a house sitter. When you're out in the bush or hopping from continent to continent, mail has a hard time catching up.

His disinterest in the house—his almost paranoid dislike of the house, he admitted—could have been a factor. Despite his rationalizing, he still felt something was off-kilter. But he didn't really care. Let the agency handle the matter. Then he wouldn't have to see her again.

That's a relief, Clint thought, driving on. Regina Flynn was a peculiarly bothersome woman. Downright unsettling in some respects. Just as well that their paths wouldn't cross again. He was a rolling stone, with little time for a relationship, however brief.

And it would have to be a relationship, he thought sardonically; one look into those green eyes and any man would know that. Not that he was interested. Nor could he be, even if he had wanted it. When it came to feelings, he was as arid as the desert.

So let the agency earn their money. They'd force her out; the Realtors would move in; end of story. He'd be out of here in no time. With a decided air of relief, he drove under the porte cochere of a fine hotel and reached for his Stetson.

Oh hell! Clint hit the steering wheel with his fist. His hat was still on a desk, in the house he'd slammed out of in a fit of righteous wrath.

Now what? Returning to the house would be absurdly anticlimatic. Yet he needed the hat. It was his lucky hat, a link with home that kept him focused regardless of where he laid his head. But if he did return, he'd have to face his pretty intruder again, and that thought raised hell with his ego, for he was astonishingly conflicted.

Regina. He tasted her name. A soft, dulcet name. A bit regal, like her. Gina. Even sweeter. All that gorgeous hair. Those absurd glasses perched on that aristocratic nose. Incredibly sexy. Which was neither here nor there, he reminded himself, making a U-turn. He had to have his hat.

As he retraced his route, another prickly question presented itself; what was he going to do when he reached the house? Just unlock the door and walk in? After all, it was his house.

"And give her another heart attack?" he muttered, recalling her fright.

Ring the doorbell, then. Request your hat, thank her and leave. Above all, don't be drawn inside.

With a start, Regina realized she was sitting in the shadowy haze of dusk. Light from a tall, automatic pool lamp streamed through the Palladian windows, glossing even the most ordinary object with silvered radiance. Obstinately blind to its beauty, she snapped on a table lamp and tried to pull herself together. She hated feeling like this; she'd done no harm to Clint Whitfield. But there was no reasoning with herself. Giving up, she searched for absolution in physical activity.

Sweeping the floor, while satisfying in one respect, did not stop the thoughts surging through her mind

much like the flames had surged through her house.
She shivered, remembering that traumatic day.

The disaster had felt so overwhelming. Afterward,
still in shock, she'd lain in her rented sofa bed at night
and had little panic attacks trying to formulate a work-
able plan for the future...

Regina's skin goose bumped as the image of flinty
blue eyes pierced her mind. Would Clint Whitfield
sympathize with her fearful anxiety? Or would he
scorn it as a weak attempt to justify her decision to
move into *his* home?

Suddenly swamped with misgivings, she dropped
the broom and began pacing. When she found herself
standing outside the master bedroom, she opened the
door and snapped on the light. Ordinarily this was forbidden territory; she would not invade private space,
although she'd peeked, of course. But tonight she felt
a perverse need to do more than just peek.

Bottom lip held firmly between her teeth, Regina
stepped inside his bedroom. She didn't much like it.
It was too dark, too ornate. An antique mahogany ar-
moire dominated an entire wall. A large rolltop desk
held a cluster of ancestral pictures in heavy silver
frames. Positioned on a somber Oriental rug, two tall,
straight-back chairs upholstered in shadow-striped silk
flanked a round, claw-footed table. All family heirlooms, she suspected; probably cost the earth. But
she'd have nightmares sleeping in that bed. The tow-
ering four-poster with its heavy velvet canopy was
straight out of a Gothic novel.

Shivering, Regina stepped back into the hall and
pulled the door shut. Going into his bedroom was a
mistake. What was the matter with her? She had to
think about her problem, not the cause of it! But the

image of a tall, rugged stranger filled her mind. *Sable hair, tousled as if by yearning feminine fingers. Sky-blue eyes that crinkled when he smiled...*

"Oh, for heaven's sake, Regina, when did you actually see him smile?" she hissed, exasperated at her silly musings. "Just a stretch of facial muscles, that's all it was. Because you yelled like a banshee and he was scared to death you'd do it again."

Still muttering to herself, Regina swept into the kitchen and turned on the stove. She needed to eat, and to heck with Clint Whitfield!

After putting on a pot of salted water, she unpinned her hair and let it swirl around her face in a rambunctious blaze of defiance. Then she slumped down on a bar stool. "Don't be a goose, Flynn," she admonished. "You can't afford pride—there's Katie's expenses to think of." Her school was supported by private donations, plus steep fees from parents. But Regina was well paid, and with careful planning, was managing fine. Until her home and possessions became ashes in that ravenous blaze...

Regina's sigh reflected her inner conflict. Right or wrong, there was no denying that living in Clint Whitfield's home had cut her expenses to the bone. But he'd gotten a break, too, she contended; regular house sitters were paid a substantial fee. And come to think of it, why did he dislike this beautiful house so much? She'd sensed his negative feelings several times during their confrontation.

"Dang!" she swore, jumping as the doorbell sent its three-toned peal through the house. Switching on the intercom, she inquired curtly, "Who is it?"

"Clint Whitfield."

"Oh, Jeez!" Regina whispered, clutching her chest.

The husky male voice had sent her heart into a stunning somersault. She cleared her throat. "Just a minute!" After hurriedly smoothing her hair, she sped to the darkened foyer. The porch lights were on and she could see him through the door's etched-glass insets; tall, bare-headed, forbiddingly stern. Snatching a fortifying breath, she lifted her chin and opened the door to face him.

"Ah, Mr. Whitfield," she drawled, her puckish sense of humor surfacing like a saving grace. "Returning to the scene of the crime?"

His dark brows shot together. "This is not a laughing matter, Ms. Flynn."

"Maybe not," she agreed with a wry smile. "But I learned long ago that if you can't laugh at your problems, you're in big trouble."

He didn't smile back.

Regina sighed. "So why are you here?"

"To get my hat."

She blinked. "Your hat?"

"Yes. When I left here, I...left in a hurry." He frowned as her mouth quirked. "It's on the desk," he ended tersely.

"Oh." She stepped back. "Please, come in. After all, it is your house." Turning, she proceeded him to the great room.

At the desk, she paused to pick up the battered Stetson. It felt good to her fingers, heavy, masculine. When he took it, his hand brushed hers. The contact created an electrifying sensation.

He jerked his hand back. "Sorry. Static electricity. This dry weather. Thanks," he said, taking the hat.

"You're welcome. You know, if you hadn't slammed out of here so fast, you wouldn't have had to come back.'' Regina met his gaze with a rueful smile. ''Then again, if I hadn't lost my temper, maybe you'd have kept yours and we could have talked this out.''

She glanced at the hat he turned round and round in long, tanned fingers. Something loosened inside her. ''You think we could try again? Like calm, rational adults this time?''

Clint shoved back a lock of hair from his brow. ''Look, I'm bushed, beat, wiped out from travel fatigue, certainly in no position to bandy clever words with you. The best I can do is apologize for my hotheaded exit. I don't really think you're a squatter and I doubt you're a thief. But truth to tell, I don't give a damn if you are or not. All I want is my hat, and in due time, your absence from my house.''

''No explanation?''

His eyes narrowed. ''I said I didn't—''

''Give a damn,'' she finished for him. ''Yes, I heard. Something of a character flaw there,'' she murmured just loud enough for him to overhear.

He frowned.

Regretting her barb, Regina tipped her head and gave his rugged face a keen, probing look. A highly sensitive woman, she saw beyond his flinty blue eyes to the profound weariness of heart and mind. His spirit was deeply troubled. *And you have an incorrigibly soft heart, Flynn,* she acknowledged with droll self-amusement.

He turned his head, bringing into focus the scar slanting along one angular cheekbone. She'd noticed it as soon as he stepped into the brightly lit foyer, and wondered at the where, when, and how of it. Intriguing, she admitted, mentally tracing it with a fingertip.

Responsive to the sudden warmth blossoming in her chest, Regina reached out to rescue the Stetson from his nervous fingers. "Here, let that rest a minute. You sit down, make yourself comfortable. If you've been subsisting on airline food all day, you're bound to be ravenous, and it's an indisputable fact that I make the best spaghetti sauce in the world—in the universe, actually. The freshest ingredients, herbs I grow myself, gourmet garlic, my Italian plum tomatoes..." She kissed her fingertips. "You'll love it."

Without waiting for agreement, she replaced his hat on the desk and headed for the kitchen.

Clint stood awkwardly in place. Dammit, he should get out of here! He didn't want her spaghetti, didn't want her chatter or warm smiles. Well, part of him did. And that part acted for him, drawing him along behind her as if on a leash.

Surprisingly he really was hungry. In fact, the aromatic smells wafting from her kitchen were driving him crazy. *My* kitchen, he amended. He ran a rough hand over his face. "This isn't necessary, you know."

"I know." She pushed a button and a low, slumberous beat of music flowed through the room. "If you'd like to freshen up, the powder room is just down the hall...." She laughed, a chiming sound that brought a sliver of peace to his troubled mind. "I guess you know where it is," she finished, eyes twinkling.

In the bathroom, he found towels and washcloths neatly laid out, hand soap in a pump bottle, a tiny perfume sample, Lili, a toothbrush and toothpaste— and red, sling-back pumps, one lying on its side as if kicked off enroute. Feminine things. To his chagrin, he found the bathroom's contents fascinating. Common, ordinary things, fascinating! Confounded, he shook his head at this atypical interest.

When he returned to the kitchen, Regina handed him a corkscrew. "Would you mind opening that wine? On the sideboard. It's a bold Texas red...or so the salesman told me!"

Her chiming laugh broke out again. To his muddled astonishment, Clint soon found himself sitting on a bar stool, opening wine, watching her pleasingly competent movements. She added pasta and a bit of olive oil to the pot of boiling water. A knife swished through head lettuce, juicy wedges that she dressed with more oil, tarragon vinegar, garlic salt and ground pink peppercorns. She sliced a crusty round loaf, poured a little saucer of virgin olive oil, sprinkled in cracked black pepper. Her long, slender fingers and oval nails captured his gaze and held it prisoner.

At her request, he poured the wine. She laid place mats and napkins on the bar and they ate sitting side by side.

Rain suddenly spattered the windows, creating a disturbingly cozy atmosphere. Through the sauce's heady fragrance he caught a whiff of some faint, flowery scent. *Lilies?* It tightened every muscle in his body. He concentrated on his meal.

Regina was aware of his need for silence. He was caught in a situation that perplexed and confused him. Maybe because he was actually enjoying it, she mused. As if enjoyment was forbidden, or at least foreign to him. What had caused him to close himself up to such a degree? Touching the wineglass to her lips, she gave him a sidelong glance as she wracked her brain for details about this fascinating man. There weren't many. Mid-thirties, childless, obviously well traveled. Divorced, she decided; a man this attractive didn't run around free for long.

"Are you a native Texan?" she asked.

He nodded, his gaze slipping back to the coral-tipped fingers holding an equally elegant wineglass. "Born and raised on a ranch in the Panhandle."

A cowboy. Regina smiled at her instant conclusion. Quiet-spoken, tall and lean, with crinkly blue eyes and a battered Stetson, he epitomized the world's image of a Texan. She was even certain he sat easy on a horse. Well, so did she.

"A cowboy?" she murmured, flashing him a smile.

"A veterinarian." His plate empty, Clint wiped his mouth and expelled a long sigh. "That was delicious. Thank you."

"You're welcome. There's more if you'd like...."

"Thanks, but I've had plenty. Whose picture is that?" he asked abruptly.

Regina's gaze followed his to an alcove furnished with built-in shelves and a small writing desk. "That's my darling Katie," she answered with a soft smile.

Clint looked startled. "Your daughter?"

"No, my sister," Regina answered, chuckling. "She's fifteen. I know she looks much younger, but she's a tiny thing, very petite, barely five feet tall. She's away at school right now."

His eyebrows rose. "Private school?"

"Yes." Regina began clearing the counter. "I'll be through here in just a minute. You finish your wine in the den—we need to talk."

Hard blue eyes collided with hers but made no headway against her imperious regard. A smile flickered around his mouth. Inclining his dark head, Clint picked up his glass and removed himself to the den.

Music still whispered, more imagination than reality. Rain played on the windowpanes as if in counterpoint. He felt angry, perplexed. Being here should be harder than this, shouldn't it? But his wife hadn't lived long enough to occupy their new home.

He sat down on the couch, then impulsively stretched out his legs full length on the soft, cushiony surface. *It's my couch,* he thought irritably. *If I want to put my feet up, I'll damn well do it.* He set aside his wine. A moment later his head fell back against the stack of jewel-colored cushions. Slowly his thick lashes fanned down....

"Oh, dear," Regina murmured as she entered the room and stopped beside him. He was asleep. The tremor that started in her heart coursed through her legs as she looked down at him.

Decision time. A simple decision, really, she thought; wake him, and be through with it, or just let him sleep and ride whatever horse the morning brings.

Regina sighed, knowing her flippancy was just a cover for an awareness she'd rather not probe too deeply. Her friends all considered her to be a warm, giving, loving person, often to a fault. She didn't agree with this last assessment; the world was in such desperate need of love, how could one possibly give too much? This part of her character she attributed to, and honored for, her Italian mother. Still, while it might be admirable to have a big heart, she thought with gentle self-mockery, it wasn't all that smart.

Because it left her terribly vulnerable.

And because Clint Whitfield was the most dangerous man she'd ever met, the kind of man who touched every instinct known to womankind.

Regina pressed a hand against her breasts. She was nearly thirty and never married. She'd come close once. But when her fiancé learned that she'd assumed responsibility for Katie after their mother's death, he'd bailed out.

"He dumped you," she corrected with brutal self-honesty.

Although she still enjoyed the sensual art of flirtation, she'd become wary of deeper involvement. She doubted any man would willingly take on such a burden. A burden she could never lay down. So she'd decided she didn't need romance in her life. Friendship would do.

But this man had stirred something deep inside her, something innocent of prior experience. And he'd done it without the usual social exchanges, with little verbal or physical communication, and without using an ounce of masculine charm.

Baffled by his effect on her, Regina studied the sculpted features now softened by slumber, the challenging, provocative scar. "Yep, dangerous," she murmured, a smile touching her mouth. "Wonderfully dangerous."

Her decision having made itself, she unfolded a cashmere afghan and spread it over his long body. Vulnerable she might be, and sensibly cautious, but she was also Irish as well as Italian, which made her courageous as well as warmhearted. She wasn't afraid to take chances—as long as it didn't hurt Katie.

Regina turned off the lamp. Only the moonlight illumined his dark face, glossing it with mystery and sadness. "Good night, Mr. Whitfield, sleep well," she whispered, and tiptoed from the room.

Three

Clint Whitfield brushed at his face as if clearing away the sunlight teasing him to wakefulness. In his years of roaming the globe, rarely did he awake confused as to his whereabouts. But this wasn't the veld, the jungle or the dun-colored plains with animals flowing across its soft folds like streams of dark water. He was in his own house—and for a fraction of a second, he expected his wife to come in....

No, no. She was gone and he was alone.

Still confused, he gazed around the sunlit room, noting plants and flowers, a snowy knit shawl flung over a chair, framed snapshots on the mantel, none of them his. The center picture, a small girl riding a hand-guided pony, pricked his memory, rousing him to his new reality despite an intense desire to avoid it.

Even worse, once confusion vanished, he was left with a sense of stupidity that made him groan aloud.

Regina Flynn. Clint groaned again as her sweet face formed in his mind. He had meant to sit down, exchange a few sensible words with the woman and leave none the worse for the encounter. Instead, he'd fallen asleep. How could he have let that happen?

I've got to get out of here! Reacting to an urgency he didn't fully understand, he threw off the afghan, bounded to his feet and grabbed his hat off the desk—

"Good morning."

The low, musical greeting affected Clint like a shout. He froze, then whirled, eyes narrowing as he noted the tiny smile sweetening her lips. Yeah, just as he thought—amusement, so faint he'd have missed it had he not been immediately suspicious!

She sat at the bar, coffee cup in hand, head still tilted in humorous regard. "Sleep okay?" she asked.

Clint grunted. She wore something long and pink and looked absurdly delicious with all those messy curls streaming around her face and down her neck.

"I slept fine," he said. "I didn't intend to," he added tersely when she gifted him with another smile. "Falling asleep here was definitely not in my plans."

"You were exhausted," she said easily. "There's hot coffee—pour yourself a cup. Then go shower if you'd like. Meantime I'll get dressed. We can talk over breakfast. Nothing fancy, just bagels. Frozen, unfortunately." She dimpled. "But there's homemade strawberry jam to even things out."

She stood up. "Coffee's there, cups over here, sugar and cream by the sink," she said, and left him standing there still forming a polite but tellingly curt refusal.

Clint couldn't resist the appeal of a hot shower. After downing a cup of black coffee, he fetched his bag from the rental car and headed for his bedroom.

Opening the door was good for one of those gut-kicking pangs that life gifted him with whenever he dared think he was finally immune. Once inside, he paused for a quick look around. He'd never cared for the plush decor. But Barbara had liked it. So he'd put up with all this red velvet and carved mahogany.

But that bed... He'd never sleep in it again. Well, there were plenty of other bedrooms in the-house-that-Clint-built. Grimacing, he made a mental note to return this heirloom furniture to her family. "Should have done that a long time ago," he berated himself. Tight-lipped, he walked on to his personal bathroom, an uncluttered expanse of white tile, forest-green porcelain and sparkling glass.

The shower felt as wonderful as anticipated. After a satisfying interval, he turned it off and grabbed a towel. Wrapping it around his hips, he wiped the fogged mirror and studied himself with a crooked smile. He looked dark, dangerous, tough as nails, a well-fitting mask that had gradually formed around his features as the darkness squeezed all joy and humor out of him.

He'd lived behind the mask so long and it had served him so well, that he doubted he'd ever be free of its cynical benefits.

"Just as well," he muttered, lathering on shaving cream. He had no use for romantic illusions. Any dreams he might have had were dead, crushed by the weight of gritty reality.

Such massive destruction left a man achingly vulnerable, and cynicism, with its razor-sharp edges, made a good shield. Avoiding his own gaze, Clint finished shaving and hurriedly dressed in khaki slacks and a white knit pullover.

When he returned to the den, breakfast was laid out on the bar. Regina, clad in a smart navy suit and low-heeled pumps, motioned him to sit. Impassively he obeyed. He accepted a cup of coffee, but ignored breakfast. He'd rather look at her than eat, an unsettling discovery. He swallowed a big gulp of coffee, burning his tongue grievously. He swore, but kept it under his breath.

"Help yourself, I've already eaten," she said with another wave of her slim, elegant hand. Absently she smoothed her hair. "Mr. Whitfield, I'm sorry if I've caused you distress. I did notify you about a house sitter," she went on in a rush of words, "but I admit I might have jumped the gun a little—"

"Jumped the gun a little?" he echoed, raising an eyebrow.

"All right, I did notify you, but I didn't wait for your response. So you do have cause to be irate. In fact, you have cause to lodge a complaint with Lamar himself," she added.

With just enough irony in her smile to make that much too harsh a punishment, he thought. "But you hope I won't."

"Yes, of course. I value my job."

"But not enough to keep from risking it. Why? What prodded you into doing this?"

Her gaze dropped. "That's not important. I don't want to play on your sympathy. Not to that extent, anyway. But I can promise that I'll be out of here by tonight, with no harm done that I can see. I really have taken good care of your home during this time—"

"During what time? How long have you been here?"

Regina stuck a bagel in the toaster. "A little over a month. I moved in the last week of August."

"And you didn't tell anyone at the office?"

"No. Oh, I told Lamar I was appointing myself your house sitter, but he assumed—and I let him assume—that you'd agreed to the arrangement. I hoped, of course, that you would do so before he discovered that I'd acted prematurely," she said stiffly. Refilling their coffee cups, she picked up hers and cautiously sipped. "Again, I'm sorry."

"Why? Because you got caught?"

"No," she replied indignantly. "Well, yes. But also because you were upset by it. I apologize, and I will get out at once. It won't take any time, I only have my clothes and my garden—"

"Your garden?" His eyebrows shot up again. "You can move a garden?"

"Well, if it's in big pots, you can. Just some herbs I use often, and a few pepper and tomato plants I've coaxed through the summer heat. Not an easy job, believe me!" she said with a sudden smile. It faded, and the room inexplicably darkened.

"I suppose not." The bagel popped up. He took half, then reached for the cream cheese. "What caused you to sneak in here in the first place? There must have been some good reason to risk your job."

"There was. And I didn't sneak," Regina added with another snap of indignance. Passing him the strawberry preserves, she continued quietly, "Obviously I needed a place to stay. And here was yours, just wasting away."

"And?" he prompted. "What happened to your home? Assuming you had one."

"Of course I had one!" Regina modified her tone again. "My home burnt to the ground, Mr. Whitfield. I lost everything I owned." She shrugged. "End of story."

"I see." Clint spread preserves on his bagel. "Is that why you lit into me about 'abandoning' my house?"

"I suppose that played a part in it." She sighed. "A big part. I'm sorry about that, too. It was uncalled for," she admitted. "But your house did seem unloved. How long did you live here before you flew off to answer the call of the wild?"

Amused by her droll tone, Clint replied, "I moved in right after it was finished, stayed two months, then left for Kenya."

"Why?" she asked, driven by an unruly need to know. "A love affair gone bad—or something like that?" she ended lamely. Meeting his opaque blue gaze, she flushed. *Oh, Gina! Shut up, for godsakes!*

"No, nothing like that. I'm a widower, Miss Flynn."

"Oh!" Regina's hand flew to her mouth. "Mr. Whitfield, I'm sorry—"

"Nothing to be sorry about," Clint said brusquely. "Since we're getting into personal stuff, didn't you have insurance on your house?"

"Yes, enough to pay off the second mortgage. The contents weren't insured, however. Living here gave me a month's breathing space and I thank you for that. Anyway, I'll be gone by this evening."

"No. You don't have to leave."

Startled green eyes stared at him. "I don't? But

you—last night you were so angry at finding me here, I thought..." A smile suddenly wreathed her puzzled features. "Well, never mind what I thought. Do you really mean it? You're not mad about...well, you know."

Clint shook his head, bemused by the effect she was having on him. Something on the order of a deer mesmerized by headlights, he thought, daring another glance into her dark-lashed eyes. *Maybe that's why I'm being such a sweetheart,* he mocked his undisciplined responses. But she had a point. The service was free and no damage had been done that he could see. He didn't give a damn about the house anyway. Why should he care if she stayed in it? Besides, he had a hunch the agency would take a different view if they learned she'd supplanted a client's wishes. He had no desire to get anyone fired. Especially not someone who'd lost everything in a fire.

"Yeah, I mean it," he said gruffly. "I'm putting the house on the market and I figure your being here will help sell it faster than if it's vacant," he added, resorting to hard-nosed practicality. "So you can stay on...provided you cooperate with the Realtor in showing it, of course."

"Yes, of course." She nibbled her lip. "I'll have to think about it some."

"My presence won't be a bother, if that's what's bugging you," he said dryly. "I'm leaving town today to visit friends, then I'll be in and out on business."

"I see," Regina said, cool and crisp, even though curiosity was eating her alive. What kind of business? Where was he going? More important, when was he coming back? And would he be coming back *here?*

Clint watched her closely, intrigued by the expressions flitting across her vivid face. Catching his regard, she blushed. "Okay, I'll try it, but I don't know," she ended dubiously. "But I do thank you. You've been very kind." She stood up and extended her hand. "Well, today is Friday, a workday for some of us. Goodbye, Mr. Whitfield. Nice meeting you."

"Yeah." Clint gave a quick, hard laugh. "Same here, Miss Flynn. See you around."

Regina nodded, picked up her briefcase and hurried out to her car. Questions about Clint divided her attention as she drove to the office. How long had he been widowed? Although the subject had aroused no overt emotion, she'd sensed something beneath that hard mask, a sadness that went beyond grief.

Was he still mired in the bitterness of his loss? If so, his wife must have been the love of his life, Regina thought wistfully. "None of which is your business, Gina," she chided. But her heart still yearned for answers.

Five days passed without any sign of a Realtor. Puzzled, Regina questioned that, too. Clint had seemed impatient to get it over with, close this part of his life. At least that's how she'd read him.

He really doesn't care about this house, she concluded, hurrying in from work Wednesday evening. He hadn't even walked through it before he left. "Sad, really sad," she murmured.

Hearing the phone ring, she ran down the hall to the den and grabbed the receiver. It was Katie, wanting to talk. Regina relaxed and enjoyed the half-hour chat with her sister. Katie found astonishment and delight in everything. This time it was a whole *flock* of baby toad-frogs no bigger than her little fingernail hopping in the grass.

Regina hung up with a soft laugh. "Toad-frogs!" she chuckled. She'd started to walk away when the phone rang again. "Yes, Katie, what did you forget?" she asked indulgently.

Silence.

"Hello?" Her voice sharpened. "Who is this?"

"Clint Whitfield."

Regina's heart fluttered. "Mr. Whitfield! I'm sorry, I... How are you?" *Idiotic, Gina!* "Did you want something?" she asked, making it worse.

"Yes, I want to know why you told Lamar about this...situation between us. I wasn't going to mention it," he said roughly. "I called the agency a few minutes ago about something else, and much to my surprise, your boss got on the line and apologized all over the place."

"Yes, well, I—I confessed what I'd done."

"Why would you do a dumb thing like that?"

"Because it was the right thing to do." She sighed. "Also because I wanted to tell him myself before he found out from someone else. Being found out by you was bad enough. He wasn't too happy about it, either, raked me over the coals pretty good. But I figure I deserved it. And, too, I have a job review next week with potential for a promotion, so I'm glad to get this behind me." Silence. "Are you back in town?"

"Back in town."

"Oh. Are you still selling the house? I mean, I haven't heard from any Realtors yet."

"That's because I haven't gotten around to any yet. I've been *busy,* Ms. Flynn," he replied irritably. "I'm just passing through town, so it'll be a few days before it gets done. This Lamar seemed more a personal friend than a boss.''

The abrupt change of subject threw Regina. ''Yes, he's a friend. But also very much a boss,'' she responded coolly. ''Look, if you want to spend the night here—I mean, this is your house, so if you'd rather not go to a hotel...'' She let it hang.

''Thank you, but a hotel's fine. Well, they're calling my flight,'' Clint said.

He was relieved to find an excuse to end this disturbing contact. Pocketing his cell phone, he grabbed his bag and strode to the gate. Why had he made that remark about this Lamar person? Who cared if he was boss or friend?

Sinking into the roomy, first-class seat, Clint closed his eyes. He was on his way to Los Angeles for a fund-raiser. *Big White Hunter pulls 'em in,* he thought sardonically; he'd never harmed anything in his life. The scar didn't hurt his image, either. Well, he was using his looks and imaginary reputation for a good cause, garnering money for the preservation of animals, which he liked a damn sight more than people.

Regina Flynn. Green eyes, a lush, full mouth, saucy little nose. He accepted a magazine, determined to put her image from his mind. Odd how persistent it was. Giving up, he stared out the window, wondering if he should just call a Realtor, save a trip back there again. That would probably be a smart move, given his annoying interest in his new tenant.

Clint relaxed, relieved by his decision. He'd call first thing in the morning, ask the agency to recommend a reliable Realtor. Maybe even ask good ole Lamar himself, he thought with biting humor.

* * *

Sunday afternoon Clint Whitfield came home again. He'd had a grueling weekend and was looking forward to some rest and relaxation. "So why am I back here?" he muttered, ringing the doorbell. Irritably he stopped his questing mind. It *was* his house.

"Yes? Who is it?" came a sweet voice through the intercom.

"Clint Whitfield." Hearing her surprised little "Oh!" touched something in him. "May I come in?" he asked testily.

"Yes, of course. I'm out by the pool. Come on in," she answered so breathlessly, he smiled.

Unlocking the door, he strode through the house and out to the raised deck, where he stopped to grab a breath. She was all legs. Bare, shapely legs. She wore some sort of garment that fell to midpoint on her thighs. He wondered if she wore anything beneath. His chest tightened. He made his way down the steps more slowly than intended.

"Hello!" she called, waving one slender arm.

"Hello," he replied, pausing on the last step. He didn't think she wore a bra, either, and that played hell with his libido. His throat felt inordinately dry. Clearing it, he continued, "Isn't the water cold this late in the year?"

She laughed. "A little. But it's ninety degrees today, so that helps keep me warm. Come on down, I'm having a little picnic, and there's enough for two." Turning, she walked to a small, wrought-iron dining set.

He followed behind her, looking for some line or strap against her back that might indicate a bra. *Damn, Whitfield! You'd think you'd never seen a seminude woman before!* Annoyed at himself, he sat down opposite her and accepted a beer. She'd placed a tray of fruit, cheese and crackers on the glass-topped table. Wondering why he was so ravenous when he was with her, he filled a paper plate.

"I just got in a few minutes ago," she was saying. "Katie was here for the weekend, but I had to take her back early, because her very best friend in all the world is having a birthday party. You can't miss an important occasion like that!" she declared, laughing.

Her face glowed, a breeze played in her loose hair, and those eyes were luminous emeralds. Clint felt something entirely unwelcome stir in his chest. It was a shifting sort of feeling, like a tiny earthquake opening up to expose something soft and vulnerable to the glare of sunlight.

"No, I guess you can't." He swigged the icy beer. "What kind of school does she attend? A boarding school?"

"No. Well, yes, I guess you could call it that. She lives there full-time. Katie's mentally handicapped, Mr. Whitfield—"

"Clint."

Regina swallowed. "Clint. We were lucky to be accepted by this school," she continued.

"Why is that?"

Delighted by his seemingly real interest, Regina described the school, a huge, sprawling complex boasting living quarters, fully staffed greenhouses, ceramic studios and a shop that showcased student handicrafts. "Leaving Katie was a wrench—I've always been so protective of her, and I miss her, her impish laughter and ever-ready hugs...."

Clint, watching her closely, noted the sparkle of tears on her lashes. "How does Katie feel about it?"

"Happy. She loves the staff and considers them simply an extension of family. Since we don't have much family left..." Regina shook her head. "Our parents died when she was quite young, so there's just Katie and me."

Clint frowned. "And you were how old when you assumed full responsibility for a handicapped child?"

"Twenty-two. Thank goodness I already had my BA in business. Her school is supported by private donations, plus steep tuition fees paid by parents. But I have a good job, so we're managing just fine."

Rising, Clint walked to the edge of the outsize pool, where a waterfall rushed down artfully placed stones. Magnificent boulders created nooks for lacy ferns and scarlet impatiens. "Why don't you have someone sharing the load? Like a husband."

"I haven't found men all that eager to share the load," she answered wryly. "Almost got one to the altar once, but he developed cold feet at the last minute."

Suddenly aware of how personal they were getting, Regina sat down and opened a cola, sipped it, glanced at him from beneath lowered lashes. His thick, dark hair curled at his nape, ruining his stony image, she thought with secret amusement.

"That's a rotten deal you've been handed, caring for a handicapped child alone," he mused. "Must have been tough."

"Oh, no, you misunderstood me. My darling Katie is the sweetest, most lovable person I've ever met. Caring for her has made me what I am today. And I happen to like who and what I am," Regina asserted. "I really don't need a man to help me do what I enjoy most in life."

Clint's mouth twisted. "Bully for you, Ms. Flynn."

"Regina," she corrected softly. "And I wasn't boasting, I was merely stating a fact." Ignoring his skeptical glance, she walked up beside him, her shoulder almost touching his. "So pretty," she murmured, gazing at the waterfall. "You'd think you were in the tropics. You did a fine job, Clint. I've never seen a lovelier pool."

"Thanks." It was almost a grunt. Clint couldn't help it—the irony of her remark had sliced like a knife. This elaborate pool had been one of several negative issues in his marriage. His wife had kept making costly changes to the original plans. With her income and trust fund, she could afford it. But he couldn't, and he'd wanted to build her the house *himself*.

A romantic gesture? More like foolish male pride, he reflected moodily. Like a moron, he had allowed resentment of her money to abrade their relationship. That it now belonged to him was another bitter irony.

Beside him, Regina shivered, and he was acutely aware of it. "Are you cold?" he asked tersely.

"A bit chilly. That breeze," she said with a vague smile.

Looking down at her, Clint felt another fluttering of something deep in his chest. For a dangerous instant he was gripped with the urge to take her in his arms and warm her.

Don't be stupid, Clint! He inhaled, filling his nostrils with her sweet, fresh scent. "Do you want to go in?" he asked in the same tight voice.

"No, not yet. Let's sit down, have a bite to eat."

Clint followed her back to the table. Cheese and crackers were remarkably unappealing; he wanted a juicy hamburger, cooked rare, perfect with just the right amount of mustard, cheese and onions. A double-decker, he thought, his mouth watering. Damn, but she had gorgeous legs. He gripped the back of the chair.

"Look, I think I'll just run along, get myself settled in a hotel, then have a real meal. Not that your offer isn't appreciated," he added quickly. "But I need a stiff drink and some red meat to erase the taste of airline food."

"You're staying in town tonight?" Regina stood up, her pulses flaring as he turned to her, those sky-blue eyes almost startling in contrast to his dark, brooding face. "Clint, you know you're welcome to stay here—"

"No," he said quickly. "I have a dinner date to-night, probably be late getting in…." Clint reached for his Stetson, remembered he hadn't brought it in, nodded again and strode across the deck to the back gate.

Wistfully Regina watched him go, her heartbeat slowing to normal as the fizzy excitement he'd created faded into the twilight.

Loneliness suddenly enwrapped her like a cold, damp shawl. As usual, the only arms she had to warm her were her own.

Four

Later that night Clint sat in a posh restaurant renowned more for its notable clientele than its food. Trying to focus on what his dinner companion was saying, he gave a surreptitious glance at his watch. His drink hadn't been the panacea he'd expected and his appetite had disappeared long before his steak arrived. He felt tired and dull. And regretful, for his companion was all sweet earnestness as she detailed her very good ideas for a local fund-raising affair. An animal lover, she was also one of the city's leading lights. He'd do well to honor her suggestions; in addition to her society position, she was a friend of his former mother-in-law.

All of which should keep his eyes open and his attention focused, he admonished himself, smothering a yawn. Idly he wondered if Green Eyes had eaten anything besides cheese and crackers...

Green Eyes? What the hell! When had his mind given Regina Flynn a nickname? And why had he forgotten to tell her that he'd hired a crew to pick up the master bedroom furniture? That's the reason he'd gone to the house. *Yeah, right,* an inner voice mocked.

Clint drained his glass and motioned to the waiter for a refill. The blonde seated across from him was still talking, her manner more relaxed than when they'd begun the evening. She was very attractive, but all he felt was appreciation for her interest in his projects.

Another yawn caught him unawares. She noticed. Abashed, Clint touched her beringed hand. "Caroline, I'm sorry I'm such a dullard tonight. Blame it on jet lag," he said with a dry laugh. "In the past week I've been from one side of the world to the other—I don't know how many time zones I'm working through!"

After she agreed to reschedule their meeting, and he was finally in his quiet suite, Clint found himself wide awake, bristling with nervous energy and no way to expend it. He might have been able to get close to his lovely dinner companion; certainly there'd been a rapport there. But cheating on the woman he loved was not part of his value system....

Clint gave himself a sharp shake. The woman he loved was dead. "Cheating's not an issue anymore, Whitfield," he muttered. Why did he keep forgetting that? Pacing, he checked his watch; ten-thirty. Would the worrisome Ms. Flynn be in bed by now?

The picture accompanying his thought perturbed him. He erased it and dialed her number with a forceful reminder that this call was legit. He had to sort out personal items from heirlooms before the furniture truck arrived.

Her soft hello caused him to cough.

"Regina, I apologize for calling so late, but I need to meet you at the house tomorrow. What time would be convenient for you?"

"I have quite a full day tomorrow, but I can meet you after work, say around six?" she replied.

"Five," he said arbitrarily.

"Five," she agreed. "I'll be waiting."

Over another obstructive lump in his throat, Clint confirmed the appointment and thanked her. Replacing the receiver, he sank into a chair and rubbed his face.

Five o'clock. She'd be waiting. Feeling terribly vulnerable, he fought the urge to pursue that thought.

But his moment of weakness had consequences; he was suddenly drenched by a wave of nostalgic yearning. Memories rode its crest like bits of floating wreckage on some dark sea. Clint bounded to his feet, his heartbeat a sickening thud. His hands clenched as he felt the familiar ache in his gut, the sting of burning eyes. Tears would have helped, he supposed, but there weren't any tears. There never had been. Crying was not something he did.

Taking a deep breath, he slammed down the containment wall again. Behind it lay a snarl of emotions he could never untangle, nor did he want to try, despite his Kenyan friend's advice. *"Hey, buddy,"* *his friend had said gently, "You're gonna have to open up and look inside yourself one of these days, confront what's in there."*

"What if nothing's in there?" *Clint had retorted, only half in jest. His terrible loss had left a deep, gaping hole in his heart. Vast areas of his being had simply dried up, a desert where nothing grew. He felt nothing, wanted nothing; he simply existed...*

Correction, Clint reflected grimly, striding to the window to stare blindly at Houston's impressive skyline. He felt something all right. A sorrow too deep to touch, a guilt immune to reason.

Survivor guilt, according to a psychiatrist friend; not uncommon and entirely unwarranted. But that didn't stop it.

Turning from the window, Clint unbuttoned his shirt and tossed it on the floor next to his open suitcase. When his long, tight frame was finally in bed, caressed by fine linen sheets and lulled by the firm, pillow top mattress, he closed his eyes. Spots danced behind his eyelids; one became a heart-shaped face with a saucy nose and dimples that flashed neon bright when it smiled....

Clint slept. And dreamed.

The next day Clint found himself again following Regina Flynn through his foyer. At first he had feared the house would trigger too many painful memories. But it hadn't. Maybe because she provided such a distraction, he thought, annoyed, which seemed to be the only way he *could* think around her. Another proper business suit showcased her curvy figure and her fraying chignon rained red-gold curls around her delicate ears.

"The entire bedroom doesn't go?" she asked, nose wrinkling as she turned to face him.

"No. I have a few things in there." Clint's voice matched his taut muscles. Desire burst free of restraints and smoldered within him like a grass fire on the verge of a becoming a blaze.

Engrossed in his own responses, he nearly bumped into her when she stopped in front of the closed bedroom door. For an instant her hair touched his face, soft, silky, exceedingly pleasant. Her scent teased his nostrils. He couldn't place the perfume, but wildflowers came to mind.

He cleared his throat. "The movers won't be here until tomorrow, worse luck. But this needed doing, so might as well get to it." *God, you sound priggish, Whitfield!* "I appreciate your help," he added, opening the door.

Drawn shades and draperies darkened the room. Clint snapped on a light, casting a peach glow over the bedstead, the carpet, Regina's upturned face. A little lick of flame flared in his groin. Swiftly he suppressed it. Stepping away from her, he turned on another, more utilitarian lamp. "This lamp and the bedside lamps are mine. The Tiffany floor lamp goes, as does the bed, chiffonier, writing desk, those two wing chairs...."

"Maybe it would be easier if you just tell me what doesn't go," Regina said.

He grimaced. "Right. That desk and chair, the television set, the bookcases and books, the lamps I've already mentioned.... I guess that's it."

"This beautiful Persian rug?" she asked, indicating the object by stretching out a long, lithe leg and hose-clad foot.

"It goes," Clint said shortly. When had she taken off her shoes? "Well, I guess that's it. Didn't take as long as I thought it would. You didn't get in trouble leaving an hour early, did you?"

"For you? Of course not." She gave a quick laugh. "You're the 'big kahuna' right now. Your wish is our command, I'm told."

"Well, fortunately for your company, my wishes are few and easily filled," he said dryly.

"Fortunately for *me*. I'm in charge of you, remember?" Regina felt a quick thrill as he grinned at her sassy response. When he did that, his hard features softened and he was catch-your-breath, drop-dead handsome. Suddenly her tongue seemed to fill her whole mouth.

Swallowing hard, she turned to open the closet. "You have quite a few clothes in here. Don't you need them?"

"No. I travel light."

She shut the closet. "How long were you married?" The question just popped out.

"Seven years."

Absently Regina sat down on the bed, clinging to a bedpost as her bottom slid on the satiny spread. "Was it a happy marriage? It must have been, for you to grieve for so long."

"I'm not exactly walking around in sackcloth, Regina. But yes, it was a happy marriage." Clint's tone flattened as doubt cast a shadow on his declaration. *Happy for the most part,* he added silently, prodded by a keen sense of self-honesty. Although he had adored his wife, there were times when he'd wondered if they were really right for each other. They had so little in common....

"Yes, you are."

"What?" he blurted, confused by Regina's assertion.

"Well, maybe not sackcloth, but for a fellow who travels light, you're carrying around some pretty heavy baggage. I'm a very sensitive woman, Clint. I see through doors and around corners," she ended mischievously.

Clint's response was a masculine grunt.

Regina slid down from the bed and smoothed her skirt. "Well, looks like we're done here," she said brightly. The pulse fluttering madly at the base of her throat made her sound breathless. But Clint had reached out to assist her off the bed and his hand brushed her breast, a thoughtless, almost insubstantial touch, but a touch nonetheless.

"Sorry," he said.

"No problem," she answered in the same light tone. But he'd felt it too, she thought, elated. His swift intake of breath belied his insouciant reaction to the brief, intimate contact. Preceding him to the door, she walked straight and tall, her entire body aware of the potent male presence behind her.

"I'm going to fix a bite to eat," she said as they reached the great room. "Won't be much, but I'd love to have you…stay…for supper," she finished on a snap of self-exasperation. "No trouble at all," she waved away his protest. "Sit down here at the bar and talk to me while I fix something. Tell me about your great adventures. How you got that scar, for instance."

Obligingly Clint took a bar stool, a bit surprised that he was doing this, but apparently he was, so he told her about the scar. "I was going down to the river one pale yellow morning, alert for crocodiles that might be lying in wait for a breakfast about my size, when this enormous lioness leaped from the brush, knocked me down with one huge paw…" He grinned at Regina's wide-eyed regard. "Actually, I was sewing up a tiny lion cub we'd found in the bush, and I guess I didn't sedate the little bugger enough, because he reached out a paw and slashed my face. So my veterinarian friend had to sew me up while I finished stitching the lion."

He grinned again. "See? The real thing never outdoes imagination. That's what I bank on when I attend these fund-raisers."

Regina gave him a querulous look. "When you say you bank on it...well, that sounds sort of unethical."

"It sounds like letting people think what they will, making it more exciting for all involved and raising lots of money for vitally needed animal sanctuaries. The sad truth is, Regina, that people need more motivation than selflessness. They need a hook to hang a fantasy on, however tenuous that hook is."

"Huh," she muttered, still unconvinced. "So how'd you come to go live in Kenya?"

"I have a friend, a vet like me, who's been doing really great work there." Clint paused as she slipped off her jacket and hung it over the back of a chair. Her movements pulled the creamy satin blouse snug against her breasts. "Exciting, too," he continued a beat too late. "Not only does he stitch up lion cubs and careless friends, he chases poachers and goes after injured animals, either to salvage, or destroy, whichever's necessary."

Catching her grimace, Clint added hastily, "If an animal's too badly wounded to save, it must be destroyed, for it's a danger to anything that crosses its path. Pretty dangerous for the hunter, too, I might add. I've had a few hair-raising face-offs with wounded animals. But I've loved working in Kenya. I love the land, the people, those magnificent animals."

Regina, buttering slices of bread, glanced at him with an inner softness she could have done without. "It really helped you cope, didn't it? That's when you went to Africa, isn't it, after you lost your...your love?"

"Yes." His brusque response closed the subject. Clint eyed the mound of bread. "What are you fixing?"

"Grilled-cheese sandwiches." Adding cheddar slices, she placed the bread on a hot griddle. Clint shook his head. "What?" she asked. "Grilled-cheese sandwiches too plebeian for your tastes?"

"After some of the things I've eaten in the bush, grilled-cheese sandwiches sound like caviar," Clint said wryly. The delicious aroma of toasting bread tantalized his nose. "You really don't have to do this, you know," he stated, annoyed again, though at what he couldn't have said.

"Do what?" She took a plastic bag from the refrigerator and unzipped it.

"Feed me every time I come over."

"I just don't like eating alone, that's all." Placing the sandwiches on two plates, she garnished them with a plump dill pickle, and heaps of radishes, carrot and celery sticks. "Eat," she ordered.

As he knew they would, the sandwiches tasted wonderful. "Comfort food," he said over a mouthful that went down like honeyed wine. "Mom used to make this for me and my brother when we'd come in from school on a winter's day. This and canned tomato soup. I thought nothing in the world could beat that combination."

"I know what you mean. Mine is a bowl of spiced pecans and sweet dark fudge. Better than sex." She sighed. A second later roses bloomed in her cheeks as she realized what she'd said. "I forgot drinks," she threw out. "What's yours?"

They settled for icy colas. Regina ate methodically, tasting nothing; her rapid heartbeat interfered with taste as well as logic. An amateur photographer, she mentally framed his face in the viewfinder. She'd love to photograph his eyes, just his eyes—smoky blue eyes—right after lovemaking. The image that brought to mind sent a hot, icy shiver streaking down her spine.

Clint looked up just then and caught her sensuous smile. Their gazes locked and something wild and sweet flared between them.

"Clint." Her husky protest had the opposite effect, drawing them closer, closer, until his warm breath bathed her lips. A piercing ache shot through her. Instinctively she moved toward him, a gasp escaping her lips as his firm mouth touched hers for a sweet, tantalizing instant.

She wanted to expand the slight contact. She wanted to catch his face and kiss his sexy mouth hard and again and again, wanted to feel the excitement of his embrace, his hands in her hair, to twist until his fingers were hopelessly entangled....

The doorbell rang. Jolted, Regina jerked back and tried to fill her lungs with sanity-restoring air. Quickly Clint moved away from her. Scrambling for composure, she stood up. "I'll get it."

"Who could it be?" he growled. "No one knows I'm here."

"Well, Clint, I have friends, too, you know!" Smoothing her clothes and hair with quick, nervous fingers, she hurried into the foyer and opened the door.

A petite, exquisitely dressed and coiffed matron stood under the porch light. The two stared at each other in mutual surprise.

"Who are you, and what are you doing here?" the woman asked, placing a hand on the door lest Regina consider closing it.

"I—I'm Regina. And I live here." Regina's voice strengthened. "May I ask who's calling?"

"Kathryn?" came Clint's startled voice over Regina's shoulder. "Well, how are you! Lord, it's been a while! Come on in. Oh, this is Regina Flynn and she does indeed live here. She's a house sitter. Regina, this is Kathryn Brandt, my favorite mother-in-law," he said, laughing as he hugged the older woman.

"I'm glad you still think of me that way," Kathryn Brandt said, patting his cheek. "Although I doubt you thought of me at all, since you didn't even bother letting me know you were home. I had to learn it from a friend. From Caroline, to be exact."

An arch smile thinned Kathryn's mouth. "She seemed quite taken with you, my dear!"

"No matchmaking—that's my number-one rule with friends and family alike. No setting me up with marvelous women with good teeth and great personalities," he warned.

Regina listened to his warm voice with an inner ear that paid no attention to superfluous things. "Excuse me," she said, smiling. "I have a kitchen to clean. Mrs. Brandt."

Inclining her head, Regina left them alone. *His mother-in-law. He'd said it so naturally. But she isn't, now, is she? Or did one stay an in-law when death, not divorce, separated a couple? And isn't it wonderful that he likes her! Men and mother-in-laws are supposedly mortal enemies.*

Her unruly thoughts raced on as Regina loaded the dishwasher and wiped off the counter. Resentment welled up again. She and Clint were enjoying the evening. *Who knows where it might have led?* an inner voice questioned. *And would you want to go there, Gina? That's mighty dangerous territory, little girl.*

"Oh, tush," Regina chided. "I'd like to at least have had the chance of deciding for myself." Grumpily she dried her hands. She hoped they'd ask her to join them, but no invitation was forthcoming. At length she gave up and went to her bedroom to change out of her work clothes.

She chose comfortable jeans and sweatshirt, nothing to hint at a trap being laid, she thought, recalling Mrs. Brandt's proprietary manner. She had liked the small woman in spite of her iciness. In Kathryn's mind, Clint was still family, so of course she'd be protective.

"I would, too, were I in her shoes," Regina murmured. Giving her hair a quick brush, she returned, barefooted, to the kitchen. Clint and his visitor were in his study and she could hear their voices but not what was being said. Maybe they'd like some coffee or something. Acting on the possibility, she walked to the closed door of the study and raised her hand to knock, when a fragment of conversation delayed her intent.

"...But you're still alive, Clint, still young and vital," Kathryn chided. "For God's sake, get out there and live!"

"Meaning find myself a good woman and settle down?" Clint gently mocked. "No. I had my shot at happiness, Kathryn. Real love is a once-in-a-lifetime thing, you know that. That part of my life is over, but that doesn't mean I'm despondent. I've got my memories, my work, my travels, good friends like you. I don't need anything else."

Regina wheeled and headed back to the kitchen, her

cheeks burning at having eavesdropped. A moment later Clint and his visitor left the study.

Kathryn gave her a long, probing look.

Regina's vague smile lit on Clint's face.

"Regina," he said heartily, "thank you for your help and for the sandwich. I appreciate it."

"You're welcome. Are you leaving now?"

Clint's blue eyes darkened as he took in the snug jeans and loose sweatshirt, a beguiling combination, he thought. Irritably, of course. Catching Kathyrn's gaze, he mentally shook himself. "Yes, we're leaving. Kathryn and I have some talking to do," he said, smiling down at the little woman.

"Yes, of course," Regina said. "Nice meeting you, Mrs. Brandt. Good night."

Regina's smile held firm until the door closed behind them. Then she slumped against the counter, battling a wave of disappointment all out of proportion to the occasion. Clint's reason for coming by tonight had nothing to do with her. His pleasure at seeing his former mother-in-law had nothing to do with Regina Flynn. "In fact, the entire evening had nothing to do with Regina Flynn," she said, the truth, but dang, that truth hurt!

She shook her head in stubborn denial. Her brain might believe that, but her heart said otherwise. Because her heart remembered the look in his eyes just before the doorbell rang and destroyed the moment. A look of hunger and need equal to her own. Or had she only seen what she wanted to see?

The next morning, Regina was just leaving for work when the telephone rang. Her breath caught; this was awfully early for Katie to be calling.

Clint's deep voice did not make breathing any easier. "Regina, I apologize for bothering you again, I don't know where my brain was yesterday, but I forgot to clean out the drawers in the master bedroom. I need to do that today, but I won't disturb you, I'll come by this morning, let myself in and back out when I'm finished."

"That's fine, Clint. Did you and Mrs. Brandt enjoy catching up on things?" Regina ventured. "She seemed very fond of you."

"And I of her. No nasty mother-in-law jokes here."

"I'm glad to hear you say that. So many men make bad jokes about their in-laws," Regina murmured. *Although I doubt that any woman she didn't approve of would have much of a chance with you.*

"In-law jokes are not one of my many faults," he said, sounding amused. "Well, all right then, I'll…see you around, I guess."

"Yes," Regina replied, wishing she could think of something clever to say. Hanging up, she grabbed her briefcase and purse, and headed for her car. *That kiss, that kiss…* The bright sunlight burned off fond illusions like wisps of fog. "That kiss meant nothing. Nada, zero, zilch. So stow it, Gina," she advised. "You can't hang a fantasy on a hook that tenuous…not if you've got a grain of sense left."

By the time she arrived at the office, she had put Clint Whitfield in a mental compartment marked *Hands Off,* and focused on her day. It promised to be exciting; today was her work review. A possible promotion, an increase in salary—all sorts of opportunities, she thought happily. Her stomach growled. "Maybe one doughnut," she allowed. And later, a traditional celebratory lunch.

She couldn't wait to share her day with Clint.

Five

By noon Regina's appetite had fled, and keeping a poker face was becoming more difficult by the minute. She'd been passed over for a promotion.

Since she was spending the afternoon checking on the competence of maid and lawn crews, she could legitimately leave the office. She drove straight home. Rushing up the steps, she barely made it inside before tears spilled over the flimsy dam she'd erected after her session with Lamar.

"Can't blame him. You did it to yourself," she berated the wet face in her bathroom mirror. "You did wrong. Did you think you were just going to waltz past that?"

Accept responsibility for your actions. Solid Sunday school logic, she thought. A vital part of her upbringing. But it didn't make the hurt go away.

The doorbell pealed. She swore beautifully. Then, wiping her eyes, she went to answer it.

"Who is it?" she asked tartly, pressing the intercom button.

"Clint."

"Oh, great, just great!" she hissed, dashing at tears. She looked a mess. "Oh, the heck with it, he probably won't even notice." She unlocked the door. "Come on in, Clint. But be forewarned, I'm not feeling very friendly right now."

Stepping inside, he said hurriedly, "I'm sorry. Something came up and I couldn't get here any earlier. When I noticed your car out front, I rang the bell." He closed the door and took off his hat. "Why aren't you feeling friendly?" His gaze sharpened. "Have you been crying?"

"No. Yes. Oh, just go do what you need to do." She turned toward the kitchen, her eyes swimming with tears. "I'll be all right...as soon as I get my head on straight."

"Why isn't your head on straight?" Clint asked hoarsely. The sight of tears on that pretty face had a peculiar effect on him. Fighting a fierce urge to pull her into his arms and soothe her hurts, he followed her to the kitchen. "What's happened?" he demanded, tossing his hat onto the counter. "Regina? What's the matter? Has someone upset you?"

Regina grabbed a paper napkin and blew her nose before facing him. "Oh, just a work thing."

"What work thing?" Clint asked, frowning as he looked into wet green eyes. The raspy lump in his throat worsened. What the hell happened to upset her so? He wanted to punch somebody. But who? "Wait a minute. Today was your work review, wasn't it?"

She looked startled. "You remembered?"

"Yeah, I remembered. So what happened?" His eyes narrowed. "Lamar give you a hard time?"

"No, not really. I—I didn't get the promotion, that's all. Nothing major, just the breaks."

"Did your moving in here have anything to do with those 'breaks'?" he asked, his voice tensing as she blinked tear-clumped eyelashes. Her head lowered, and he could see the clean part in her hair. His hands fisted as an astonishingly primal emotion coursed through him, drawing his muscles to bow-string tightness. "Did it?" he demanded.

"Possibly."

Oh, hell. "Can I do something to help?" he asked brusquely.

Yes, oh, yes, you can! Just hold me, just put your arms around me and hold me. Yes, I do need to be held! "No, thank you. Anyway, the person who did get the promotion deserved it just as much as I did, maybe more." Her chin jerked up in icy denial of the quaver in her voice. "So that's that. If you'll excuse me, I need to change clothes. I'm checking out maintenance-crew work this afternoon."

"Have you eaten?"

"No. I'm not really hungry. I'll grab something later," she said dully.

"I have a better suggestion. Let's order pizza. Let me feed you for a change."

"That isn't necessary—"

"I know it isn't *necessary,* it's just something I want to do, all right?" he asked gruffly. Tendrils clung to her damp cheeks. Someone needed to smooth them back into place. He gave his itchy fingers a wad of napkins to hand to her. "Now what do you want on this pizza I'm ordering?"

"Just mushrooms. The pizza-delivery number is by the telephone." She opened the refrigerator and took out her plastic bag of crudités. "Won't hurt to have some healthy stuff with that pizza," she said, flushing at his amused glance.

"Did I say anything to the contrary?" Clint asked. She smiled, and he looked at her with great irritation. She had the sweetest mouth this side of heaven. "I like pepperoni, so we'll order a large, get it half and half," he continued.

She nodded and emptied celery and carrot sticks onto a saucer. "Clint, you had no influence on my promotion. It was strictly my own doing. I tried to get away with something that wasn't quite kosher, and I didn't make it. My fault, my responsibility. So don't go feeling guilty about it. And don't say you're not—why else are we having pizza?"

"Maybe because I'm hungry?" he suggested, his brows drawing together in a line of censure. She laughed and he frowned darkly. She had a great laugh.

After ordering their lunch, Clint went to his bedroom. With no regard for neatness, he dumped the contents of his dresser drawers into a suitcase, then emptied the bedside tables. When he'd finished, he took a silver framed picture from a drawer, unwrapped its protective velvet cloth, and sat down in one of the wing chairs. Memories wound through the quiet room like gossamer ribbons.

"Clint?" Regina's voice brought him back to the present. "If you need some boxes... Oh, you're through already," she said, glancing at the filled suitcase. Her gaze shot to the picture he held in both big hands. "Is that…"

He blew out a long breath. "Barbara. Yes. Taken on one of our rare vacations. We went to Barbados for a week of fun in the sun." One corner of his mouth lifted. "She got so badly sunburned the first day, we had to stay indoors most of the time. But it was nice, all the same."

"I bet Barbados is wonderful," Regina murmured, her gaze still on the picture. Such classic beauty, she thought; pale gold hair, ivory skin, patrician features. "She was lovely, Clint."

"Yes. She was that. Inside and out." His voice was low, almost hoarse. Clint cleared his throat. "Well, I'm through in here. I'll just take this to the car." Sliding the picture into a handsome leather bag, he zipped it and started for the door. "Our pizza should be here any minute now."

Regina walked beside him. Her hair was slicked back and trapped in a no-nonsense chignon. The business suit was gone; now she wore jeans, boots and a tailored white shirt, belted at the waist. Three unfastened buttons allowed a tantalizing hint of cleavage. In mind-numbing contrast, she was wrapped in a calm, cool reserve that defied even the thought of touching.

Clint's mouth twisted. *Don't even think about it, Clint.* But the mockery fell flat. Because it would be sweet, sweet pleasure to muss that hairdo and wrinkle that pristine shirt. His vaunted self-control had a weak spot when it came to her. Last night had proven that. He'd almost kissed her. A real kiss, not that soft little brush of lips. How far would it have gone if the doorbell hadn't interrupted them? His hands had itched to reach for her, fill his fingers with soft curves…

He mentally shook his head at his mind's frivolous ramble. There was no weakness; he was merely reacting as any man to an elusive, challenging female.

"Clint, where are you taking that suitcase?"

"To my hotel. Where else?" he replied tightly, keeping his gaze straight ahead.

"That seems so silly, you going to a hotel when there are so many vacant rooms in this house. And your house at that. Why don't you just stay here when you're in town?"

Clint's mouth went dry again. "I'm quite comfortable in the hotel, Regina. I have a large suite, meals when I wish, laundry and maid service...."

"Well, I admit I can't compete with that. No maid service here, Mr. Whitfield. A meal now and then is the best I can offer!" They paused in the foyer. "Clint, I would feel better about this situation if you weren't left out in the cold, so to speak. Don't let me be the reason you're not living at home. I'll leave if you prefer to be alone."

"Trust me. You're not the reason," Clint said shortly. He opened the front door. "What about your reputation? I suspect you're the kind of woman who'd care what people say."

"I have a good reputation and I know myself, so what others think or say is really not important," Regina said quietly. "I would really like us to be friends. Friends who share a house. But if that's a problem, then I think I should move out."

She looked up at him, suddenly alarmed. "Clint, you're not thinking I *have* to live here, that I can't afford an apartment or house of my own, are you? Because if you are, let me set you straight right now.

I am not a charity case, I won't have to go live under a bridge if you kick me out!''

"Well, I'm very glad to know that," he drawled. "I'd hate to think of you living under bridges on my account."

Regina's mouth twitched as she tried to hide her pleasure. *He has a sense of humor,* she thought. *That's so important in a man.* The stern mask had softened, too. She wondered if he knew it. "I still think you're just being kind," she charged. "You said you were selling this place, yet I haven't seen hide nor hair of a Realtor."

"That's because I haven't engaged hide nor hair of a Realtor." Setting down the suitcase, Clint brought out his billfold as the pizza delivery truck pulled in behind his big sedan. "This place has been sitting empty for nearly three years, so what's the hurry?"

"Well, none, I guess," she replied doubtfully.

He swapped money for pizza.

"I'll take the pizza," she said. "You get the suitcase."

Clint left the suitcase in the foyer. As Regina opened the pizza box, the irresistible aroma of melting cheese and spicy sauces wafted through the kitchen and her appetite returned full force.

For a time they just ate, hungrily and delightedly, the way food should be consumed, Clint thought. Cold beer washed it down. Swallowing, he gazed at the longneck bottle as if assaying an ancient artifact. "Gina, if I did stay here…"

"You worried about that little kiss?" she asked.

Clint watched her lick one corner of her mouth, much as he'd like to do. She looked so confident, he thought, and yet so very vulnerable.

"Not worried, but...you're very attractive, Regina," he said almost formally. "I like you and I enjoy being with you. But it wouldn't do for you to get hung up on me."

"That sounds a bit egotistical, don't you think?"

He reddened. "Maybe. But I didn't mean it that way. I just don't want you to get hurt."

An elegant eyebrow arched in amusement. "Clint, a little case of lust isn't life-threatening, you know. It just adds a smidgen of spice to the friendship, that's all. Good for the libido, I hear."

Regina pressed her rosy lips to the icy longneck, green eyes dancing. "Whether or not I get *hung up* on anyone is my business and in no way concerns the person with whom I'm..." She began laughing. "That's not going to sound right, is it! Well, you get the idea."

Deep blue eyes held hers, searching for she knew not what. She must have passed inspection, for he sat back and took another slice of pizza. Regina let out the breath she'd been holding unaware.

"There is one thing, though, that should be discussed before you decide," she said. "I bring Katie home for a weekend now and then. Is that going to be a problem? Because if it is, then I'm out of here anyway, so none of the rest matters, does it!" she said lightly. But her eyes were dead serious.

"No, of course it's not a problem. I won't be around that much." Clint swigged beer, his mind racing. Living here was practical. What harm could it do? *You kissed her,* came the immediate answer. *No,* he argued. *That little buss? It was nothing. I can handle it.*

He smiled. "Well, I guess you have yourself a roommate, Ms. Flynn."

"Good," Regina said in the same light tone, although her heart raced and a crazy little refrain kept circling her mind. *He's staying! He'll be here in the morning, in the evening, at night. Why am I so transported by that? Because his infrequent smiles hold tantalizing hints of tamped-down warmth and passion. Because of the way he watches me when he thinks I'm not looking. You're nuts, Gina. Lust, remember? You're the one who termed it. And rightly so.*

But under her ironic admission lay another, darker acknowledgment. The hunger he had ignited with that little kiss was growing, fed by an imaginative fantasy she could not suppress.

She studied his face, noting the patina of experience and cynicism glossing his rugged features. In comparison, her own thin layer of sophistication seemed sadly lacking. *I don't care. I want him here!*

"Well, here's to my new roommate," she said, and clicked her bottle against his.

As the week progressed, Clint's uncertainty about his decision eased. Appointments with various organizations and corporate personnel from Houston's many large firms kept him busy during the day. Leaving early and returning late at night cut down on exposure to his house sitter.

Thursday morning, when he followed the incomparable fragrance of freshly perked coffee to the kitchen, she was eating breakfast, dressed in a long terry robe, barefoot, hair piled willy-nilly atop her head. A fetching picture, he conceded, pouring coffee since she ignored his empty cup.

"Hi, stranger," she said, tilting her head.

"Hi yourself. No more pampering, hmm?" he joked, splitting a bagel. "I'm on my own now."

"That you are, unless our schedules overlap," she returned easily. "I'm doing a pork roast tonight." Luminous green eyes crinkled in a smile. "In case you find yourself in the neighborhood around suppertime."

"Sounds good. Maybe I will find myself in the neighborhood around suppertime...which is?"

"Seven." Regina's heart skipped as she glanced at his rugged profile. He was smiling, that closed, unreadable expression he used as a shield against intimacy gone for the moment, softened, she suspected, by their bland conversation. He stood beside her, the clean, citrusy scent and sinewy heft of him filling her womanly senses with deep-down pleasure. Not even a superbly tailored suit could tame that raw and magnificent masculinity. Desire shot through her like liquid fire.

"By the way..." She stopped and cleared her throat. "You made the gossip column today," she continued, waving a folded section of the *Chronicle*. "Says you and Caroline... How do you pronounce that last name?"

"The *H* is silent."

"Ah. Were an item at Tony's Sunday night." She looked up with a bright smile. "So, are you two an item?"

He gave a short laugh. "Not that I know of. Purely business."

"Nice business, I'd say," Regina tossed off. She laid the newspaper aside. "Is that your new pickup truck out front, or a rental?"

Clint drained his coffee cup. "Mine. I got tired of

mucking around with rental agencies and the itty-bitty cars they want to give me.''

She had a charming chuckle, low and throaty.

He glanced at his watch. ''Gotta run. You can eat my bagel. See you tonight.''

Briefcase in hand, he strode outside to greet a perfect day. A day for playing hooky. The temptation was absurdly strong. Grab Regina, some food and drinks, and off to the park.

Deriding the silly impulse, he got into his shiny red truck and headed out of town on I-45, en route to Fort Worth.

Dusk was falling by the time Clint returned to Houston, tired and disgusted at the waste of a fine day. His heart inexplicably gladdened as he turned into his driveway. Welcoming lights shone from the windows, and the porch lamps were on, creating a golden path to the door for him, where she would be waiting....

Clint stiffened, wary of the effervescent warmth pervading his long frame. Always before he'd looked forward to escaping this accursed house. Now, to his consternation, a part of him was looking forward to homecoming.

But another part, the icy, dogmatic, in-charge part, swiftly checked the wall behind which he existed and found it intact. Relieved, he collected his briefcase, jacket and tie, and strode up the walk.

Opening the front door, he stopped, nostrils flaring at the delicious aromas filling the air. In the den, candles burned; in the kitchen, more candles put a sweet, sultry note into the atmosphere. He set his possessions on a chair.

"Hey," he said, helplessly smiling as Regina crossed the kitchen to greet him.

"Hey," Regina returned, lips curving as she took in the white shirt, sleeves rolled to the elbows, a vee of crisp dark hair below the open collar. Right where I'd like to place a kiss, she thought. She stopped in midstride, her gaze colliding with his. She forgot coquetry, forgot how to shield her reaction to his presence. Green eyes as honest and direct as the feelings they expressed, widened at the riotous tangle of emotions he created with just that smile.

Between thick, dark lashes, his eyes gleamed, hot as the blue gas flame that fired a furnace. Excitement exploded within her. She stepped nearer, her gaze holding his, her tongue flicking across her upper lip as if anticipating the potent demands his mouth would make. Up close, she could see the shadow of beard darkening his jaw, could, if she chose, feel that prickly growth against her own tender skin. This is madness, she warned herself. But he was sexy, exciting, dangerous. Emphasis on the dangerous, she thought, exulting in the risk.

Somewhere at the back of her mind, astonishment whispered urgently at her reckless need to know intimately the taste and feel and smell of this man. She ignored it. In blazing defiance of her own protective instincts, she rose up on tiptoe and pressed her lips to his throat.

He didn't move. For a tremulous moment Regina was pierced by doubt. She'd been so sure this sensual hunger was mutual, that he, too, felt this growing need for intimacy. Maybe she'd read him wrong—maybe he didn't find her all that appealing and she was making a fool of herself.

No! Her fingers spread over his broad shoulders. Teasingly slow and deliberate, her lips mapped the firm line of his jaw, then traced the full length of his intriguing scar.

''Clint,'' she murmured. The warmth filling the space between them shimmered with tension and flared into heat as their bodies touched. Ever so slightly he turned his head, and she felt the fierce sweetness of his mouth brushing hers.

The moist, honeyed contact was tantalizingly brief. Regina made a small sound of protest. Then, boldly, wantonly, she thrust her fingers into the sable darkness of his hair and captured his mouth in a passionate kiss.

He caught her shoulders, a neutral clasp that neither held nor pushed away. He'd gone rigid, his tall body all hard flesh and muscle. Instinctively she swayed against him, creating a blaze of friction that made him suck in his breath.

A shudder whipped through him; an instant later his arms swirled around her with delicious roughness. Before she could catch her breath, his mouth took hers with an urgency that stopped time.

Regina held on to him as the world spun in slow, blissful circles. His body heat fused with hers, making her blazingly aware of being a woman. She was awash in pleasure. Her entire being was attuned to the magnificent, taut-muscled body molding to hers.

Lost in that ole black magic, whispered the small shred of logic her mind held on to, despite her desire to totally immerse herself in this fiery delight. *Madness, Gina.* She pushed the warning away, an easy task as his mouth slanted across hers, his tongue penetrating, exploring, all wild-honey sweetness and if this was madness, it was splendid!

Then he jerked back, his embrace becoming two firm hands holding her away from him. She felt his face burrow into her hair as he fought to regain control. Not yet trusting her legs, she held on to his shoulders. Although they no longer touched, those fiery sensations still sizzled through her body.

Regaining her composure, she slowly moved back from him, until only her fingertips rested on his shoulders. She tilted her head and looked up at him. He was obviously discomfited. By what, her boldness? The gorgeous pleasure of their kiss? Was he wondering what it demanded from him? Nothing! she thought furiously.

Stepping away, she formed a saucy smile. "You're not a bad kisser for a cowboy!"

Clint blinked. "I'm not, huh?" he said, still trying to fathom her quicksilver mood as well as his own. His had priority, for he needed to rein in the wild urges surging through his embattled body. He had managed to keep his head...until she'd fitted her femininity so sweetly, so naturally, to his maleness. Even now, even with the space he'd put between them, his body vibrated with desire.

And with her looking up at him, smiling—God, the bewitchery of that smile!—he wanted, *ached,* to kiss this green-eyed goddess into melting submission.

His sharp shake of head severed that thought. *Off-limits, Clint!* He should have put a stop to this before it ever got started. But how in hell did a passionately besieged man do that? He wasn't made of stone. True, but he'd better act like he was.

Leaning an arm on the kitchen counter, he studied her with a lopsided smile. "Regina, I have no intention of getting romantically involved with you. So, given that we're sharing a house, do we have a problem?"

"I don't," Regina said. "I don't know about you, but I enjoyed what just happened. Just consider it a sort of appetizer before dinner," she continued, opening the oven door and peering inside.

Clint gave her a dubious look, but decided to take her at her word. After all, it was just a kiss. All he had to do was keep his distance. Or at least use his iron-clad control when tempted by her beguiling nearness.

"Well, then, neither do I," he said. "Have a problem, I mean. And as much as I enjoyed the appetizer, I'd like to get on with dinner. I'm starving."

He sat down on a bar stool. "Today was such a dud. When I agreed to do this fund-raising bit, it sounded easy. Everyone loves animals, right? Well, maybe they do, but animal rights doesn't have the éclat of a famous disease."

Regina smiled to herself, pleased by his openness. She took the foil off a pork roast cooked on a bed of fresh sage and rosemary, surrounded with tiny new potatoes. "Not glamorous enough, you mean."

"Yeah. To be frank, I hate it. Almost as much as I hate wearing a suit and tie. A cotton shirt, battered jeans and well worn boots—that's my style." He sighed. "Well, it'll soon be over and I'll be on my way back to Kenya. Lord, that smells good!"

Regina took a much-needed breath. "You won't be staying here at all?" she asked, reaching for a slotted spoon.

"No. There's no way I could squat on one piece of land for the rest of my life. I'm a tumbleweed now, a world traveler." He opened the wine she set out, and filled two glasses. "That description pleases me. But not my parents. I'm still a disappointment to them."

"How on earth could you be a disappointment?"

"I didn't follow their plan for me. After I got my degree I was supposed to come back home, open an office in town, marry a local girl and produce a flock of grandchildren..." He lifted his wineglass. "Instead, I stayed in Houston, married a lady who was too busy *saving* kids to *have* kids. Then, when I lost her, I ran off to Kenya instead of coming home to them, to let them share my trauma."

"Well, the last part of that sounds logical."

"I didn't want to share my trauma," he said shortly. "I still don't. It's *my* business."

Regina sliced bread and placed it beside the roast. "You didn't want children, either?"

"Yeah, I did." His somber gaze moved beyond the warm, aromatic kitchen to a darker place that held him captive for a moment. Then, with a start he came back to light and life. "But it wasn't that important," he said, shrugging. "Regina, this looks great."

"Thank you." Suddenly ravenous, Regina filled her plate. "It's kind of funny, you being a tumbleweed and I'm...what kind of weed would I be, seeing as how I'm confined to my own small plot of earth, by circumstances beyond my control?"

"You mean Katie?"

"Yes."

"I don't know." Below opaque blue eyes, a smile stretched his mouth. "Whatever kind you are, we're complete opposites."

Regina's wry smile matched his. "Yeah, you can't stay and I can't go. Can't get much more opposite than that."

Regina scooped potatoes onto their plates, her mind running back over their conversation. He'd laid it out for her with sobering clarity. No room for illusions, no ifs or maybes.

I'd find his candor far more pleasing, she thought, dishing up salad, if it didn't sting so much.

Six

The following week Clint spent on the road, often berating himself for volunteering for this fund-raising, or for what, in his secret opinion, amounted to begging for money.

Yet he sincerely believed in what he was doing, which was providing sanctuaries for the planet's dwindling animal populations. That alone was motivation to keep going. If he could arrange the purchase of even one acre held in perpetuity, he'd be doing something good for this magnificent little planet called Earth. Of course he was thinking in terms of thousands of acres. Even that wasn't enough—vast tracts of land were desperately needed. Rain forests, mountains, cloud forests, plains, tundra—so many animal habitats were in danger of being totally wiped out.

At the moment, however, he wasn't out pursuing some noble cause, he was stuck in a long line of Houston's freeway traffic, three lanes funneling into one to bypass construction. Diesel fumes, mad drivers, the infernal noise of semis—God, he couldn't wait to get back to Kenya! In retrospect, life was so much simpler there. Just daily little skirmishes with life and death, he thought ironically, nowhere near as hazardous as riling Regina Flynn.

A hard sigh escaped him as her image shot to mind. She confused him, angered him, pulled him this way and that with just a slow, teasing glance from those gorgeous green eyes. He felt certain that deeper involvement with her spelled danger, to her, not to him. She deserved warmth and affection, and he was devoid of both. Any worthwhile emotion he was capable of sustaining was superficial at best. Yet, from the beginning he'd had to struggle against the powerful attraction she exerted on him, all the while knowing that he had nothing to offer a woman like her. Why then, when he was with her, did he keep forgetting that?

Still caught up in his deliberations, Clint parked in his driveway with little recall of having gotten there. His house loomed dark and lifeless in the graying dusk. Regina hadn't yet come home from work.

As he exited the car, huge raindrops pelted him. Inside the house, he snapped on light after light, suddenly ravenous for the warmth and brightness that welcomed him when she was here.

Shedding his jacket and tie, he tossed them on a chair and walked back to the foyer, rolling up his sleeves. Wind and rain buffeted the windows. "Be nice to be able to park in the garage," he muttered. But the garage was stacked with unopened boxes, another thing on his to-do list. "At least clear enough space for Regina to park." He shot an anxious glance at his watch—it was after six. Where was she? At the tail end of his question the door opened and she fairly flew into his arms. Her slim figure surged against his body before she regained her balance. Brushing raindrops from her hair, she laughed up at him, rose-red lips curving around his name.

"Clint! Thank you for catching me—I think I'd have been blown right on through the house if you hadn't!"

Sparkling green eyes snared his with ridiculous ease. Clint forced himself to release her soft shoulders. "I'm glad you're home," he said. "It's wild out there." *And in here.* One hand, acting entirely on its own, smoothed tangled curls from around her glowing face. Her lips were naturally that soft rose color, he discovered. Immediately aroused, he swayed toward her, then caught himself and backed off.

"You're pretty wet—why don't you go get some dry clothes on while I fix us a drink?" he said with artificial ease. "What's your pleasure?"

"A peach cooler." She kicked off her shoes. "Should be a couple bottles on the top shelf of the fridge."

Clint went to the bar; she, shoes in hand, to her bedroom to change clothes. When she came back, her drink was waiting. He sipped his brandy, his quick glance taking her in from head to toe. She was absolutely enchanting in those baggy gray sweats.

"A bad day?" she asked, eyeing him over the rim of her glass.

"No, not too bad. I met several people today who are working on their own, saving maltreated or just discarded animals. It's not just exotic animals needing our help. One lady is constantly in hot water because of her collection of pets that have been abused or left behind when a family moved. I was so impressed with her sincerity, I arranged a grant from the trust for her, enough money to purchase a house and some acreage outside city limits.''

"The trust?'' Regina queried.

"The Barbara Brandt Trust. I established it shortly before I went to Kenya. So my wishes are given special consideration from the board.''

"I should think so!'' Regina said, nestling into the soft comfort of the couch.

Clint followed her lead, and both settled down with their drinks. His errant hand promptly slid across the back of the couch to toy with the loose corkscrew curls tumbling over her shoulders.

Regina leaned her head into his caressing fingers, delighting in conversational intimacy almost as much as physical touch. The weather helped, she thought, grateful for anything that loosened his tongue. There were so many things she wanted to know about him.

"Clint, how did your wife die?''

He stiffened. "A car wreck.''

Subject closed. Regina tried another tack. "So you just closed this house, sold your business and went to Africa. Is that how you dealt with such a devastating loss?'' she ask softly.

"Yes. It's the best place to at least try. Someone said that Africa is the last place in the world that still has a soul. The rest of the world has been civilized to the point of ossification.''

Stretching out his legs, Clint said, low and husky, "You should see the stars in an African sky, Gina, so many you feel awed just looking up to the heavens. Never in all my travels have I seen such glory.''

He called me Gina. "I wish I could see it. But the next best thing is having someone who has. Describe it to me." Regina sipped her drink, the liquid sweet and icy on her lips. Finishing it, she closed her eyes, her heart fluttering as she focused her senses on his moving fingers. If only they'd move downward. She imagined his touch on her breasts and frissons of excitement rushed through her. She had wondered what she was going to do about these profound feelings he evoked, especially after their frank talk that night.

You can't stay and I can't go.

Well, at least that was something she knew about him.

She turned her face to his, her voice throaty as she murmured, "Can a girl could get another drink in this place?"

He made an amused sound. "I don't know—what's your limit?"

"Two," she said, miffed that he guessed she had a limit. "After that I get all cutesy-giggly. You'd hate it."

Regina crossed her legs and languidly watched him amble to the desk to answer the ringing telephone. A moment later her languor evaporated. She jerked erect, her attention zeroing in on his caller.

"Susan!" he said with mingled surprise and pleasure. "What's up? You doing okay? I'm surprised a croc hasn't had you for lunch by now...." He laughed. "Uh-huh. You been throwing any more stones at large animals?" He laughed again, short, throat-only sounds. "What? You're kidding! Kilimanjaro? Lord, no! I've never climbed a rock, much less a mountain..."

Regina got up, took her glass from his hand and

went into the kitchen to open another cooler. Her heart ached. He sounds so warm, so unguarded, she thought. He's never been like that with me. Had he slept with this Susan person?

When he hung up, Regina rejoined him on the sofa. "A friend from Africa?" she asked lightly.

"Yes. Susan's a doctor, came to Nairobi for a six-month volunteer stint at the hospital. If you were familiar with the Nairobi hospital, you'd know what a feat that was. She's a pretty little thing, short blond hair, blue eyes... Not someone you'd think to meet out in the bush. But that's where I met her—trying to get the attention of a hippopotamus."

He chuckled. "The hippo ignored her pleas to turn around and pose for her camera, so she lobbed a stone at it. Got its attention then," he said dryly. "It turned and charged her. The two male tourists with her didn't even stop when she stumbled—it was every man for himself! Luckily the hippo lost interest."

Clint chuckled again and shook his head. "And now she's decided to climb Mt. Kilimanjaro. And she will." He swirled the golden liquor. "Quite a woman," he murmured.

"You had an affair with her," Regina said, half question, half statement.

Surprised, Clint reared back. "How the hell did you come to that conclusion?"

"It was in your voice."

Needing a respite, Clint drank brandy. "A gentleman never kisses and tells, you know."

"Oddly enough, I believe that gentlemanly bit." Regina took a bolstering drink of potent peach schnapps. "But it wasn't an affair of the heart."

"Ah. And you know that because...?"

He didn't sound annoyed. Encouraged, she replied, "Because you wouldn't allow it. It was strictly physical. You've closed off that part of yourself. Falling in love would be—"

"Impossible," Clint finished for her. "And don't knock the physical—it can be very sweet, very special, between two consenting adults." His eyes glinted. "As long as each knows the perimeters of an affair, it can be magic."

"I'm sure it can." Regina took another mouthful of courage. She looked at him, a quick, nervous glance— any second now he would tell her to mind her own business. And be justified doing it. "But why is love impossible?"

Clint sat back, relaxed and at ease. "Because experience has taught me a valuable lesson," he replied mildly. "Love can tear a man apart. It can, quite literally, leave you without a reason to live. Only, you do, because you're too tough to crumble like a cookie. You just go on, that's all." A slight shudder passed through his shoulders. "No sane man would expose himself to the possibility of such anguish again."

"But wasn't it worth it, Clint?"

The softly voiced question struck him a visceral blow. Suddenly aware that he was in danger of losing control of the situation, he stood up, drained his glass and set it aside. "That's getting a little too personal," he replied coolly. Grabbing his hat, he turned toward the foyer. "I'll be late, so don't wait up."

"Don't worry, I won't," Regina said, so angry and hurt she could barely hold it in. Where was he going? And why? Tears stung her eyes. Furiously she rejected them.

Clint, standing tall and straight, head held arrogantly high, strode on. He gripped the doorknob. A moment ticked by.

"I didn't sleep with Susan...although why it should be any of your business is beyond me." He jerked open the door to face a maelstrom of wind-driven rain. "This is stupid," he said, and closed the door.

"I think so," Regina agreed, her anger evaporating in the sweetness of relief.

Why am I acting this way? she wondered. What do I care whom he sleeps with? He's right. It isn't any of my business. So why am I *making* it my business? Can I be falling for him? No, of course not. Don't be a goose, Gina, she scoffed with a tinge of desperation. You hardly know the man.

He came back into the room, stopping at the bar to pour another brandy before moving to one of the rain-lashed windows.

Regina couldn't stand the silence. "So why did you tell me if it's none of my business?" she asked, her gaze tracing the long lines of his body. Broad shoulders, trim waist and hips...a great derriere, she thought, licking a drop of schnapps off her upper lip.

"I don't know. Maybe you made me feel guilty."

"Why in the world should you feel guilty?"

"Who needs a reason?" he retorted. Catching Regina's frown, he capitulated. "I'd been widowed a little over a year when I met Susan. Being attracted to her was natural, I suppose. She's a captivating woman, sweet natured, intelligent, absolutely fearless. But desiring her felt too much like betrayal. Just too soon, I guess." He shrugged. "Have you eaten?"

"I—uh, yes, I stopped for a burger on the way home," Regina stammered, her mind still ensnared by his revealing response. "But I can fix you something if you're hungry."

"You don't mind?"

"It would be my pleasure."

"Thank you." Clint turned back to the window. Her throaty reply had reached deep inside him and stoked the many little wildfires she'd started. How could she do this to him? How could she bring him to this state of arousal with only a word, a look, a smile? Damned if I know, he thought, his sardonic grin directed at himself rather than the one responsible for his inner agitation.

Regina was softly humming. He sat down at the kitchen counter. It offered a better view than the window. "Grilled cheese again?"

"No. Ham and cheese. On white bread, though," she said, slicing a tomato. "That's the only kind I find edible."

"The worst kind," Clint said, and they bickered amiably while he ate.

Afterward he thanked her, excused himself and went to his room. Since the master bedroom had no bed, he'd taken the blue-and-white bedroom two doors down from Regina's. Seated in a comfortable chair, he watched television, a two-hour documentary that at least killed the time he found heavy on his hands. It also kept at bay all the questions churning up his mind.

A great wave of yearning swept over him, so strong it would have knocked him off his feet had he been standing. "Oh, nonsense," he muttered. But the desire tightening his torso wasn't nonsense. He wondered if she was asleep. What did she wear to bed?

This particular wonder in no way cooled his fevered body.

* * *

Midnight. The rain stopped and moonlight sprayed a silver streak across his bed. Clint flopped onto his back again. Insomnia was nothing new; rarely did he sleep more than four hours a night. He ought to use this downtime to sort himself out. But he didn't know where to start.

"I bet she'd know," he muttered, folding his arms beneath his head. The rain began again, increasing his unrest. He closed his eyes, imagining himself back on the Serengeti, alone with just the stars for company. But for all his self-imposed solitude and penance, sometimes he got lonely. Sometimes he craved. And what he craved lately, he admitted, feeling angry and cornered, was Regina.

Sweet, guileless Gina. He couldn't get free of her. At night she tormented his dreams. Daytimes, her image glowed at the back of his mind like a night-light someone forgot to turn off.

A sound outside his room snagged his attention with the acuteness of a barbed-wire fence. Was she awake, too, her lithe body tossing and turning, restless, needful? "Oh, hell, Clint, cool it, will you?" he muttered disgustedly, listening so hard his ears crackled.

Regina put down the book she'd been trying to read for the past half hour. The rain sluicing down her windows had a wild, lonely sound. Like the tears of a broken heart, she thought, adding her sigh to the night's turbulence. A glance at her clock evoked another sigh. Midnight. The witching hour. The man she wanted with every fiber of her being slept just down the hall.

Resigned to wakefulness, Regina left her bed and

made her way to the kitchen without turning on a light. Her pensive mood required softer illumination. She lit a tall, thick candle. Perfect. Just enough to guide her through the great room to the French doors. Opening one, she stood perversely enjoying the fresh, clean air chilling her arms and shoulders. *You should have put on a robe,* she chided the unruly part of herself that had coaxed her from bed. The thin straps of her equally thin, floor-length gown provided little warmth.

She closed the door and lay her forehead against cool glass as melancholy overwhelmed her. A sob tore loose, tears scalded her cheeks. *What do you want, Gina?* she demanded. The unequivocal answer chilled her even more than the night air. *I want him.*

Her mind raced back to the scene in the kitchen. He'd felt something for this Susan, but his sense of betrayal, as if he'd be cheating on his wife should he yield to sexual desire, had kept their relationship platonic. Mulling that over, Regina felt a sweet warmth pervade her innermost core. That Clint still cherished his wife's memory was a plus, not a minus; it was gratifying to know that a man could love so deeply. Perhaps, in time—

Regina stilled with a splash of shock as footsteps padded across the parquet floor. *Like I wished him here,* she thought, holding her breath to discern his location. He was standing behind her.

Hurriedly she wiped her cheeks. "I hope I didn't wake you."

"No, I couldn't sleep, either." His hands touched her upper arms. "You're cold," he accused. Grabbing the cashmere afghan from the couch, he enfolded her in its luxurious warmth.

His hands, Regina noted intensely, stayed curved

around her shoulders. When she let herself relax, his body heat seeped into hers, dispatching the chill, increasing the warmth from inside out. Unmoving, lest it disappear, she closed her eyes and reveled in the sheer pleasure of standing here like this.

"Were you crying?"

That sounds like an accusation, too, Regina thought wryly. "A little. I was…homesick, I guess, thinking about my house, how much I miss it. It was a nice house, nowhere near as grand as yours, but still, a very nice house." She sniffled. "I miss having a family, too."

"You don't have any other relatives?" he asked gruffly.

"Distant relatives, most of whom I've never even met. So I didn't bother calling them when…when me and my little shadow were left alone in a suddenly big, frightening world." Regina leaned her head back and felt the delight of a solid shoulder pillowing its weight. "But we're okay. Katie and I are doing just fine. And someday, if I'm lucky, I'll find someone to complete our little family circle. That's my dream. A family of my own. Did you ever dream that dream?"

Silence.

"I'm sorry, that was rude of me—I forgot that you…that you…" Regina couldn't finish it.

So he did it for her. "Had that dream and lost it? Yeah. And it was nice while it lasted, but you'd better not pour your whole self into it. Because that self gets horribly mangled when it ends."

"Losing her must have been terribly traumatic," she ventured.

"Traumatic?" Clint gave a harsh laugh. "It damned near killed me."

"I'm so sorry you've had to bear such pain, Clint,"
Regina said, soft and low. She felt his lips touch her
hair, and knew intuitively that if she turned her face
to him, he'd kiss her. A kiss she literally ached for.
*But it would be a pity kiss, I suspect. Sympathy, em-
pathy, whatever. I don't want it.*

Even while she worded the denial, her body sought
the exciting warmth of his. Bonelessly soft with desire,
she leaned back into his hard, muscular strength with
a murmurous little sound of pleasure.

Seven

Clint Whitfield thought he knew every nuance of desire, every little stirring in the dark, secret places of a man. He was wrong. Nothing had ever moved him as much as Regina's soft warmth nestling against his embattled body. It signified a level of trust much deeper than anything he'd encountered in his adult life. She felt so fragile, like fine crystal, he thought, letting his mouth delight in the clean scent of her hair. Silken strands slipped between his lips, seducing his tongue to join in the erotic play.

Experience had taught him how to deal with passion's persuasive power. Why then, was he having the devil's own time keeping his hands off the source of his exquisite torment?

She gave a little shrug, just a movement of one shoulder, really, and the afghan slipped to the floor, leaving only his arms to warm her. Clint sucked in a breath, feeling her femaleness with every masculine sense he possessed. Flawless, peach-gold skin, tiny straps crisscrossing her shoulders, black satin fabric clinging to her supple body. The wonder of Gina.

Outside, the rain poured down. Thunder raged, and jagged streaks of lightning pierced the blackness. Inside, the storm's energy electrified the very air he breathed. Clint muffled a groan as her round little bottom touched sensitive male flesh. Doggedly he tried to resist the powerful attraction she exerted. But then she turned her face up to his, and resistance melted like snowflakes in summer. He took her luscious mouth in a long, deep kiss that set him on fire.

Somewhere, in the small part of his mind not engaged utterly in this delicious contact, alarms sounded, urging his return to reason. *She could get hurt.* Heart pounding, he tried to draw back with a terse apology. But the look on her lovely face dragged him right back into it. She turned in his arms, face-to-face, head thrown back, exposing her delicate throat for his pleasure. Then he was holding her—oh, it felt good to hold her! Drawing her closer, feeling her curvaceous body fit into his as if made for that purpose, destroyed the last of his defenses, and very soon, his ability to think.

Head-spinning moments later, she pulled free with a tremulous laugh. Taking a much-needed breath, Clint attempted to clear his head, and failed. For she was kissing him, his chin and cheeks, his ears, down his neck and back up again, tracing his mouth with her tongue, licking, nibbling and then hotly kissing.

His control severely strained, hands clenched in her hair, Clint said hoarsely, ''Regina, listen…'' He fought for air. ''Gina, you know where this is going. Are you sure you want—''

Her lips stilled his voice.

Casting off restraints, glorying in the freedom to make love to this captivating woman, Clint kissed her with hot, exultant pleasure. The space between their bodies pulsated with erotic tension. Unable to wait any longer, he swept her up in his arms and headed for his bedroom.

Her throaty laughter tantalized with sublime promises. In his temporary quarters, he set her on her feet, then stood mesmerized as she slowly slipped the thin straps of her gown off her shoulders and arms. The fabric slithered down her hips, to fall in a shimmering pool around her bare toes. His breath stopped as he drank her in. The high, uptilted breasts, the stunningly ripe curve of hips, the fluff of curls between her thighs and that lioness mane of red-gold hair drifting around her naked shoulders. Sultry green eyes gleaming between thick, sooty lashes, rosy lips parting in a slow, sensuous smile. Oh, the wonder of her!

His breath, when he remembered to breathe, was ragged. "Regina. Oh, you are lovely," Clint half whispered. He still stood in place, his gaze locked upon her wild Irish beauty, his mind and heart engaged in chaotic battle. "Are you sure, Gina?" he asked again—and for the last time, he vowed.

She tipped back her head, masses of curls streaming down her slender back, a hand on one hip. "I'm sure," she said, and Clint's battle was over.

Clumsy-fingered, he began unbuttoning his shirt. She helped, undoing a button, kissing his exposed chest, laughing up at him.

"Driving me crazy," he accused. He'd always considered lovemaking a serious thing, to be *taken* seriously, blast it! But she continued to charmingly provoke, tease, tantalize, with her lips, her fingertips, her smile. How he got undressed was a mystery to Clint. But eventually he stood, all arrogant nudity, for her inspection.

Regina ran two fingers down his torso, touching him with mind-numbing intimacy. Unable to take any more of this glorious torture, he swept her up again, high in his arms, feeling ten feet tall and strong as an oak.

Suddenly her boldness vanished. Eyes like tender flowers looked up at him; her soft mouth trembled. Reacting with fierce and awesome gentleness, he laid her on his rumpled bed and came down beside her.

"What do you want of me, Gina?" he asked, unbearably husky.

Regina gave him a sweet smile. "Just exactly what you're doing, Clint. Only more of it," she added with an impish sparkle in those green, green eyes.

He regarded her for a moment as if puzzling over something. Impatient, burning with the need to touch and be touched, Regina reached for him—and gave a startled gasp as he responded. His hands were suddenly everywhere, caressing, seeking, finding, his mouth following the trail blazed upon her heated skin. Shock waves of pleasure washed through her, inducing another gasping moan. Incredibly aroused, she slid her hands over his powerful shoulders, urging him down to her.

His weight was a delicious burden upon her yielding body. The need to be one with him melted bones and willpower alike. She couldn't get enough of his hungry kisses. As she moved with him in the age-old dance of love, Regina felt a deep, joyous singing in her heart. This is so right, so beautifully right, she

An Important Message from the Editors

Dear Reader,

Because you've chosen to read one of our fine romance novels, we'd like to say "thank you!" And, as a special way to thank you, we've selected two more of the books you love so well, plus an exciting Mystery Gift, to send you absolutely FREE!

Please enjoy them with our compliments...

Pam Powers

P.S. And because we value our customers, we've attached something extra inside...

Peel off seal and Place inside...

How to validate your Editor's
FREE GIFT
"Thank You"

1. Peel off gift seal from front cover. Place it in space provided at right. This automatically entitles you to receive 2 free books and a fabulous mystery gift.

2. Send back this card and you'll get 2 brand-new Silhouette Desire® novels. These books have a cover price of $3.99 each in the U.S. and $4.50 each in Canada, but they are yours to keep absolutely free.

3. There's no catch. You're under no obligation to buy anything. We charge nothing—ZERO—for your first shipment. And you don't have to make any minimum number of purchases—not even one!

4. The fact is, thousands of readers enjoy receiving their books by mail from the Silhouette Reader Service™. They enjoy the convenience of home delivery...they like getting the best new novels at discount prices before they're available in stores...and they love their *Heart to Heart* subscriber newsletter featuring author news, horoscopes, recipes, book reviews and much more!

5. We hope that after receiving your free books you'll want to remain a subscriber. But the choice is yours— to continue or cancel, any time at all! So why not take us up on our invitation, with no risk of any kind. You'll be glad you did!

6. Don't forget to detach your FREE BOOKMARK. And remember...just for validating your Editor's Free Gift Offer, we'll send you THREE gifts, absolutely FREE!

GET A FREE MYSTERY GIFT..

YOURS FREE!

SURPRISE MYSTERY GIFT COULD BE YOURS _FREE_ AS A SPECIAL "THANK YOU" FROM THE EDITORS OF SILHOUETTE

Visit us online at
www.eHarlequin.com

- Two BRAND-NEW romance novels!
- An exciting mystery gift!

PLACE
FREE GIFT
SEAL
HERE

YES! I have placed my Editor's "Thank You" seal in the space provided above. Please send me 2 free books and a fabulous mystery gift. I understand I am under no obligation to purchase any books, as explained on the back and on the opposite page.

326 SDL DC3H

225 SDL DC3D
(S-D-OS-08/01)

| | | | | | | | | | | | | | | | | | | |

NAME   (PLEASE PRINT CLEARLY)

| | | | | | | | | | | | | | | | | | | |

ADDRESS

| | | | | | | | | | | | | | | | | | |

APT.#   CITY

| | | | | | | | | | |

STATE/PROV.   ZIP/POSTAL CODE

Thank You!

thought with soaring delight. *Whatever he wants I will give…*

She meant to dilute that reckless vow. But reality vanished in blissful pleasure far beyond anything she'd known, a deep, driving intimacy that fragmented her being. And then came a whirlwind of ecstasy that gathered the scattered shards of Regina Flynn, and knit them together again in perfect order. *Yet, there was a difference, an unnamable difference…*

Regina closed her eyes, trying to clarify that disturbing thought. *A superficial difference, if at all,* she decided, even while she clung to the only stable thing in her universe, the long, muscular lines of Clint Whitfield's body.

She remembered thinking, at some point, how beautifully right this was. Was it? At the time it seemed that way, but now…

The soft breath she exhaled stirred his hair. Sighing, he moved down until her breasts pillowed his head. Helpless to resist, she kissed the dark, damp locks. She wished she knew what he was thinking. This all felt so eerily natural to her. Did he feel it?

The questions kept coming, but there were no answers. When he moved off her and pulled her close against his solid warmth, she exulted in the small gesture. But she wished he'd say something.

A short time later, she heard his breathing change. He was asleep. *Since I can't figure this out by myself,* she thought, *I might as well go to sleep, too.* She couldn't, of course. Her hyperactive mind would not shut down. *He'll be gone soon.* The warning scattered like rose petals blown by the wind, too insubstantial to dwell upon. He was here now, and that's all that mattered. Because *now* was real.

Cuddling deeper into his encircling arm, she inhaled the dark, intimate scents wafting around them. His, mine and ours, she thought puckishly.

Curving one leg across his hips, Regina slept.

Morning dawned tender-blue and gold. Regina came awake with a start as memories of last night flooded her mind. Her wakening gaze shot to his side of the bed. Empty. No sounds came from the adjoining bath. Maybe he'd gone back to his personal bathroom. Climbing out of bed, she grabbed her gown and wrapped it around her nude body. "Clint?" she called softly. Then louder, but he didn't answer.

"Because he's not here," she muttered, closing the master bedroom door behind her.

In her own room she slipped on a housecoat then hurried to the kitchen. The aroma of fresh brewed coffee filled the air, but still no Clint. Shoulders slumping, Regina poured a cup of coffee and walked to the French doors looking out on the pool. Its waters glistened Caribbean blue, but no dark head ruffled the surface. "Face it, Gina, he's gone again."

Pondering his absence, she wondered if he'd wanted to avoid facing her. Had their night together been more of a failure—his failure—than something magical? In some confused way, had he, in his mind, cheated on his wedding vows?

Like unsupervised clothes-hangers in a dark closet, questions bred questions. The only answers were what she came up with. "Which is zilch," she muttered.

It was Saturday, so she leisurely bathed and dressed, thinking she'd go out for breakfast, then drive down to pick up Katie for the weekend.

Clint hadn't mentioned his plans. Stepping outside

into searingly bright sunlight, Regina was even more certain that he'd gone off to avoid that discomfiting "morning after."

Straightening, newspaper in hand, she turned to go back inside when a florist's truck wheeled up the driveway. Puzzled, she shaded her eyes against the blaze of sunlight and waited. The young man exiting the truck carried an enormous bouquet of roses. Exquisite roses, white blushed with pink, long stemmed, wrapped in waxy green paper tied with a resplendent pink bow. "For me?" she asked.

For her.

Taking the flowers inside, Regina eagerly opened the little envelope and stood for a moment absorbing its message. "Thank you for a beautiful night, Regina. The rarity of that kind of pleasure makes it even more priceless." It was signed with a flourishing *C.W.*

A lovely sentiment, she thought dryly, but what did it really say? That he'd enjoyed their lovemaking? "Well, duh, Clint," she muttered. Enjoyment was a given. She'd held nothing back from him.

"Well, maybe he didn't want that much of Gina Flynn," she whispered, her eyes misting. But the flowers were lovely, a round, closely packed circle of fragrant pink blossom. She buried her nose in satiny petals and inhaled their matchless scent. She had to get a grip, regain her steady grasp on life, a life that now included Clint Whitfield, in whatever shape or form that inclusion took.

In late afternoon Regina sat beside the pool watching Katie play in the hot tub. It was unbelievably warm for this late in September. Clad in a sleek black maillot and sunglasses, feeling marvelously languid, she let her gaze sweep the area. Her "garden" was in need of replacements. Yellow and bronze chrysanthemums, she decided. An old-fashioned swing in that lovely sunroom would be great....

That thought brought to mind another: why hadn't the house been shown yet? Clint hadn't mentioned selling since the first week they'd met. Had he changed his mind? Had he decided to stay on in Houston, at least for a while?

"Dream on, Gina," she said sardonically. "You know he's going back to Kenya as soon as he finishes his business here. He left no doubt about that."

A tall shadow loomed over her and she looked up in alarm. "Clint! I didn't hear you come in!" *Oh, Lord, did he hear me talking to myself?*

"Sorry, I didn't mean to startle you," Clint said.

"That's all right." Regina tensed as his gaze swung to the hot tub. Hurriedly she stood up.

Clint's focus was heavily conflicted, torn between Regina's loveliness and the incredible girl in the hot tub. He knew instantly who she was, and that knowing shook him, an internal shock that clawed at his heart.

"Katie, this is Mr. Whitfield," Regina said, lightly clasping his arm. "Clint, this is my darling Katie."

"Hi," Katie burbled, lifting a small hand in a cheery wave. Tilted green eyes sparkled at him beneath a fringe of black bangs. The cap of loose, fluffy curls was perfect for that heart-shaped face, Clint thought.

He cleared his throat. "Hi, Katie, glad to meet you." He inclined his head. "My God, she's beautiful," he murmured to Regina, who nodded mutely, her face glowing with love for her precious little sister. He felt choked with outrage. That Katie was indeed beautiful—those green eyes, snub nose, rosy bow of a mouth—was killingly poignant when reminded of her handicap; the sparkle in her eyes was spirit, not intelligence.

"She's also very sweet," Regina confided. "Can you believe they wanted me to commit her to an institution? According to so-called experts, she'd be better off in the care of professionals who knew how to deal with children like her."

Flushed with indignation, Regina continued. "These *experts* said she wouldn't learn, *couldn't* learn even the most basic functions, such as dressing and feeding herself, combing her hair. But I refused to accept that. It's true there are many things she'll never be able to do—I'm not blind to her shortcomings. I just want her to be all she can be."

Regina's hard sigh made Clint aware of the profound sorrow she bore without so much as a whimper. To be left with this lovely, handicapped child, to assume the role of guardian, parent, sibling—God, how had Regina done it? He felt a sudden need to sit down.

"Meeting her is a shock, I know," Regina said softly, sitting down beside him.

"Yeah, it is," he replied huskily. "When you hear the term *mentally handicapped,* you just don't expect such exquisite beauty to be connected with it. It's so unfair, so damned *unfair!*"

He inhaled, his voice roughened by the emotions coursing through him. Feelings were anathema to Clint. But here they were, mauling him like a rampaging bear. *Get a grip, Clint!*

"I don't know how the hell you bear it!" he burst out again.

"The same way you bear any grievous thing. You

just do,'' Regina said matter-of-factly. ''Taking it one day at a time makes good, solid sense when your whole world crumbles. If you try to plan ahead, think too far down the road, your brain shuts down. So you take solace from the small things—putting breakfast on the table, doing laundry, brushing her hair, reading bedtime stories…the life-saving force of small, mind-numbing tasks. They support you, until you can stand up to your fears.''

Regina gave him a sidelong glance. How was he taking this? Did he like her darling Katie? And how was he equating last night with meeting her face-to-face? In that instant Regina knew, deep down in her fast-beating heart, how terribly important his reaction was.

Clint's hand covered hers. Her burden was even more appalling now that he'd met Katie. He wanted to do something, fix something, just act in a manly, heroic way, damn it! *You're no hero, Whitfield,* his inner voice jeered. Clint winced, wanting so much to challenge the scornful charge. But he didn't, though it abraded his pride to admit his inability to comfort Regina.

''You guys hungry?'' he asked abruptly. *When in doubt, go to food,* he mocked his muddled self.

''Well, of course we're hungry!'' Regina was saying. ''What did you have in mind?''

Clint ran a hand through his hair. He had nothing in mind. ''A burger, cheese steaks, hot dogs, Tex-Mex, you name it.''

Regina's eyes took on a soft shine. ''You want to take us to dinner?''

Clint caught the subtle emphasis on ''us.'' *What the hell are you doing, Whitfield? Getting involved, that's what,* his mental sentry hissed. Tenderness ambushed him as his gaze locked with the green-eyed elf in the hot tub. "I like hot dogs," she confided.

"Well, then hot dogs it is!" he said heartily, then formed an exaggerated frown. "You're not going like that, are you?"

Katie giggled. "No, of course not!" she said with great disdain, clambering from the pool to enfold her petite body in the huge towel Regina held. She was still giggling as they went inside.

All that evening Clint covertly watched the engaging girl. His heart wrenched each time he looked into her eyes and noted the vacuousness lying behind her sparkling gaze. That she giggled, hooted, laughed out loud bewildered him. Didn't she know what a rotten hand life had dealt her? He couldn't pinpoint what so outraged him. All he knew was that his gut twisted every time he thought of such gross injustice.

He reminded himself that it was none of his business. Nonetheless the situation gnawed at him.

During their chatter-filled meal, on another level of his mind Clint was factoring in the use of his house with the two sisters' welfare. Regina would box his ears if she knew he was thinking like that, he mused. That starchy pride of hers wouldn't easily accept pity. Imagining her on the dole made him laugh to himself. She was courageous, high-spirited, a willow able to sway, not break, with every ill wind. Even so, it was a tremendous responsibility to shoulder alone.

I guess I'm just going to have to help her. Without getting involved any deeper than I already am, he added, struggling to quell the many little stirrings in his heart.

One was the wonder of last night. Whenever he

dropped his guard, images welled up with stunning force, filling his mind's eye until he could barely swallow the succulent hot dog.

Catching sight of himself in a mirror, the center of this domestic little scene, constricted his throat even more. He was out of his element. Way out, he added grimly. But there was still the prickly matter of tonight; where he was going to sleep?

He glanced at Regina's quiet face. She had thanked him for his roses, said they were lovely and that he shouldn't have, but offered no clue to her frame of mind. It had been all he could do to keep his hands on his food and not her, while she was all polite smiles and sweet courtesy.

He responded in like manner, which made for an awkwardness he hated, but felt helpless to combat.

On the drive home, tension filled the front seat, muted, because Katie was chattering. She loved his truck. Regina laughed and patted his hand. It was their first real touch of the evening. He caught her slender fingers and threaded them through his.

Desire whetted his need to hold her close. Later, he told himself. When we get home.

But at home he was left to entertain himself while Katie was bathed and tucked into bed. He'd never been so aware of time's passing, slowly, edgily, each moment stretching out in an eternity of questions.

At last, hearing Regina's footsteps, he turned from the darkened window with a helpless smile. She'd changed her slacks and shirt for a silky blue kimono sashed tightly around her trim waist. Damp hair tumbled around her shoulders. His gaze held hers as he stepped closer and touched her face.

The sweetness of her mouth drew him like a bee to

honey. But, sensitive to the wariness in her demeanor, he picked up her hand and began kissing her fingers, one by one, in silence.

Slowly drawing her nearer, he brushed kisses on her mouth, her cheeks, her ears, her lovely white throat, feeling the pulsing life beat under his lips. Her eyes closed, but she didn't react to his advances save for a quick breath that emerged as a gasp.

Defeated by her passivity, he leaned his forehead against hers. "Talk to me, Gina."

"I'm sorry, Clint. I just feel so... Why did you send those roses?" she burst out.

"To say thank you, to tell you how much I—what it meant to me. Why do you question them?"

It was Regina's turn to flounder. "I thought...well, it seemed like some sort of... I thought you were trying to avoid the 'morning-after' scene. Like you didn't want to face me, so you sent roses in your stead. Or as a sort of payment," she added, lowering her lashes.

"Good God—payment?" he rasped, rearing back. "Tell me you didn't really think that."

Regina expelled a long breath. "No, I didn't really. But I try to be honest with myself regardless of how unpleasant that might be. And the possibility was there, small, yes—okay, teensy-weensy," she defended herself against his scowl. "But I do think you didn't want to face me."

"I didn't know what to say," he replied. "You're different, Gina. I've been a bachelor for many years— experienced, I guess you'd say. But none of the old tried-and-true stuff works with you. I don't want to mislead you—I'm bending over *backward* not to mislead you. I know you value honesty as much as I do."

"Yes, I do, and I think that's very sweet," Regina

said, touching his cheek. "I'm sorry you had to suffer my kid sister and me tonight."

"Now what the hell are you talking about!" he exploded, grabbing her shoulders. "I asked you two out to dinner—"

"But you didn't enjoy it, and don't say you did," Regina snapped as disappointment stung her eyes. "The camaraderie was so artificial—"

"It was, I agree, but surely you see why? I was in over my head, Gina. I don't know how to talk to little girls like Katie. But I tried."

"Yes, you did, and I thank you for your valiant effort," Regina said with a dry laugh. "As for tonight, which I think is on your mind as much as mine, Katie sleeps with me when she's here, because my bed's familiar to her. I've limited our intrusion to that one bedroom and bath, and the public areas here."

"Oh, dammit, Gina! You know you're welcome to use the whole house. Give her a bedroom of her own. Fix it up for her in ruffles and bows or whatever teenage girls like these days."

"Thank you. But the existing arrangement suits us both. She feels comfortable, and I feel good, knowing I'm providing her with a sense of security. Well—" she checked her watch "—it's only nine-thirty, but I'm beat. In truth, I feel like I've maneuvered my way through a minefield tonight."

"So do I," he said, nuzzling her ear. "Did we just have a fight?"

"I guess we did." A smile flickered across her lips. "Now comes the making up, or supposed to. Are you going to be around tonight?"

"I'll be here," he said.

* * *

Midnight came and went before Clint's light turned out. He lay on his back, arms folded beneath his head, replaying the evening again, with the same results. His confusion stemmed from such a tangle of sources impossible to sort through it. So he drifted back to the glowing memory of last night.

More confusion. Their lovemaking had been so deep and passionate, it shook the very foundations of his being. Yet, despite such consuming ecstasy, he'd tried to hold himself emotionally aloof. As he had attempted to do again this evening, he acknowledged, and with the same lack of success. Small wonder, he thought; every time she smiled at him, he felt that treacherous stirring in his heart....

Gradually his eyes closed—only to pop open again as his bedroom door opened. In the moonlight she looked like a temporal being in her long white robe. He heard the rustling of fabric, then felt a nudge against the mattress as she felt her way. A wild river of joyous excitement coursed through his body. "Regina?" he murmured, beginning to smile.

"Yes, it's me. I decided the making up should come sooner rather than later. Are you in the mood to make up, Clint?" she asked throatily.

"If I'm not, I'm sure you can change that...."

The bedsprings creaked.

"Oh, yes," Clint said huskily. "I am definitely in the mood."

Eight

Clint awoke around eight the following morning. Surprised to have slept so long—and so soundly—he glanced at the empty pillow next to his without surprise. Of course she'd be up and gone by now. Listening hard, he could make out the murmur of feminine voices drifting down the hall. The sounds fell sweetly on a man's ears, he acknowledged, a soft smile thinning his mouth.

A quick self-appraisal found him edgy and confused, which was nothing new, he thought sardonically. But physically he felt great. Last night had been the kind of sexual magic every man dreams of and few find.

Bounding out of bed, he stretched, then put on his jogging clothes. October had come riding in on a cool front, which, in Texas, was anything below ninety degrees. Smiling at his small jest, he laced his shoes, then hurried to the kitchen.

Katie looked up with a tentative smile. He winked at her, then glanced at Regina, who looked edible in a cuddly pink robe. He wanted to gather her into his arms and hold her close. Bury his nose in her hair and inhale its moist, delicious scent. Instead, he smiled at both winsome females.

"Good morning, ladies. Katie, Regina." His voice lowered to huskiness as he looked at Regina. "Jogging," he said when she raised an eyebrow. "The fitness center has an air-conditioned track."

Giving his handsome physique an exaggerated once-over, Regina nodded. "I'd say you've made regular use of it," she said just to him, then raised her voice. "I'll fix us breakfast when you get back, but Ms. Katie's hungry now."

"I can wait," he replied. The urge was too great; stepping closer, he kissed her brow. "Until later."

She laughed, green eyes glowing. "Until then."

Still feeling good, he stepped out into a blue-and-gold morning too beautiful to enjoy quietly. He began whistling.

Regina's expression grew pensive as she watched him leave. Pouring Katie a glass of milk, she asked jovially, "Well, do you like our new friend, Clint?"

"Yes. He's a nice man. Is he going to live with us all the time?"

Caught off guard, Regina gave a nervous laugh. "Oh, I don't know about that. And you're not to ask him, either, you hear?" Poking a straw into Katie's glass, she ruffled the girl's crisp black curls. "But you're right. He is a nice man. Okay. I'm going to go get dressed, honey. You finish your breakfast, then watch television until I get back.''

Accustomed to obedience, Regina left the kitchen without concern. She felt wonderful, sleek as an otter, she thought with a saucy grin. Last night's bliss quota was off the scale.

Lost in thought, she stripped off the robe. It was disturbing to acknowledge how eagerly she'd watched for some sign of bonding between Clint and Katie. Throwing them together hadn't gone so great, she conceded. But it hadn't been all that bad, either. True, Clint had been a trifle ill at ease in the crowded family restaurant. Once he'd adapted to the noise level, though, he did fine.

She wanted to think he'd even enjoyed himself, but at the back of her mind doubts swarmed like summer gnats. She tried to ignore their annoying buzz. ''You know what I think?'' she chided the image in her mirror. ''I think you think too much.''

Donning shorts and a sleeveless sweater, she drew her hair into a ponytail and tied it with a green ribbon, then returned to the kitchen.

It was empty, as was the great room.

''Katie?'' No response. Regina's arms suddenly goose-bumped. She felt the emptiness of the house like a physical weight.

Telling herself not to be a ninny, she dashed back to the bedrooms to check again, with the same alarming results.

Fighting panic, she ran outside, across the deck and around the entire length of the pool, her heart in her throat as she searched the clear blue water. No Katie. Breathing easier, she probed through the shrubbery lining the fence and flower beds. All was peaceful and quiet on this lovely Sunday morning.

Oh, God, where is she? Tears splashing her cheeks, Regina tore through the house again, upstairs and down, calling for Katie. Silence. Where else to look? She jumped as the doorbell rang, then raced to answer it, thinking, *Katie! Oh, you little scamp, you're in so much trouble....*

Jerking open the door, she said furiously, "Katie, I ought to... Oh, Clint, it's you!"

"It's me," Clint agreed. "Sorry to disappoint you, but I forgot my key." His grin faded as he took note of her wet eyes. "Regina? What's wrong?"

"Oh, Clint, it's Katie—I can't find her anywhere! I left her watching television while I got dressed—I hardly took any time, and when I came back to the kitchen she was gone! I've looked everywhere and I can't f-find her!"

"Gina, shh, listen, listen to me," Clint said, grasping her shoulders. "We'll find her. Just calm down. She probably just wandered off."

"No, you don't understand, Clint. She's just a little girl. She doesn't know the area—she has no more idea of getting around out there than a six-year-old!" Regina said frantically. "I've looked everywhere—I even searched the pool. Nothing there, thank God."

She drew a shuddering breath. "I just can't imagine where she could have got to! Maybe we should call the police. Or is that hysteria talking?"

"An excellent idea," Clint said. "I know a few people at the station. Let me handle it."

Wildly agreeable, Regina managed to stand in one spot while Clint talked with a policeman named Ray, apparently a friend. "It's probably nothing more than a child wandering away.... She's fifteen. Mentally handicapped. A little girl, Ray," he stressed, heavily aware of Regina's attentive presence. "No, she's not familiar with the area.... Short black hair, about four foot ten, yellow shorts and top. Right. Thanks."

Hanging up, Clint took her tightly clasped hands in his. "He's going to check around the neighborhood, and I'll do the same. You stay here and wait by the telephone. And stop worrying. She'll turn up, I promise."

"Bad things do happen, Clint," Regina said, infuriated by his soothing manner.

"I know they do, but not to you," he replied, squeezing her hands. "We'll find her."

On that note of assurance he strode out the door. "Wish I could be as sure as I sounded," he muttered, only too aware of the hot, hollow ache in his chest. He was compelled by one thought; this was Gina's treasure and no harm must befall her.

Barely half a block down the street, he pulled to the curb with a sizzling oath. "She's on foot, Clint, not driving around," he said, turning his anger inward. Swiftly he parked and began walking down the sidewalk calling Katie's name. Since privacy hedges enclosed most of the houses, he figured she'd hear him before he'd see her.

He figured right. From a house across the street, Katie came running over the velvety lawn with a cat in her arms.

Behind her came a worried lady speaking in broken English. When Clint answered the maid in Spanish, she responded with a torrent of relief. She didn't know Katie. But apparently the girl had crossed the street, chasing the calico cat now squirming in her grip.

Clint felt a jagged burst of something between wanting to hug Katie with all his might, and shaking her
until her teeth rattled. It was a very peculiar feeling.
Shaking his head in wonder, he thanked the woman,
then persuaded Katie to give up her cat and leave with
him.

But she refused to get into his car. She'd been
taught never to get into anyone's car without Gina's
permission, she said stoutly.

"Okay, we'll walk, then," he agreed. To his surprise, she slipped her hand into his and walked beside
him, chattering about cats and the possibility of getting
one for herself.

Regina came flying down the steps to meet them.
"Katie!" she cried, catching her close. "Oh, honey,
are you all right? What on earth got into you," she
asked furiously, "wandering off like that! I ought to—
to…" She hugged Katie again. "Oh, my little love,
I'm so glad you're all right!"

Clint watched their reunion with furrowed brow.
Scolding Katie, hugging her, half laughing, half crying, Regina put into action the peculiar feeling he'd
had. "I'll be damned," he muttered.

Raising his voice, he said, "From what I can gather,
a cat ran across our patio and she chased it, all the
way out the driveway and down the street."

Smoothing Katie's flyaway curls, Regina looked at
him with wet green eyes that somehow managed to
open a similar wellspring inside him. He coughed,
frowned, mumbled something or other when Regina
instructed Katie to thank him, and she did.

"My pleasure," he said gruffly. "Now if you'll excuse me, I'll retrieve my truck. Then I'll get out of
these sweaty clothes. And you, young lady," he said

to Katie, "stay away from stray cats. One of them might decide to eat you, and then what would we do?"

Katie giggled and ducked her head.

Regina caught his arm. "Thank you, Clint."

He harrumphed. "You're welcome."

"When you get back I'll fix us a splendid breakfast," she called after him. "Oh, shouldn't we call that policeman, tell him Katie's been found?"

"I'll take care of it," Clint said.

After getting a hyperactive Katie settled down with coloring book and crayons, Regina turned on the oven. Opening a can of biscuits, she slid the pan into the oven, then cleared away the remains of her sister's breakfast.

When Clint came in, she smiled at him with her heart in her eyes. He carried his Stetson. Jeans, a cotton knit shirt and polished cowboy boots completed his breath-stopping ensemble.

Katie whispered something to her sister. Regina laughed. "Katie wants to know if you're a real cowboy!"

"Well, as a matter of fact, I am. I even have a horse at the ranch, named Turtle," Clint said.

"Turtle?" Regina echoed. "Not much of a name for a handsome stallion.... It is a stallion, isn't it?"

"He knows he's a handsome stallion," Clint defended the old swayback roan he used to ride.

Regina leaned to Katie's urgent whisper, then laughed again. "No, Katie, you can't ride his horse!"

Her pulse quickened as her gaze focused on Clint's clean-shaven face. "Ready for a big breakfast?" she lilted.

"No, don't bother, Regina."

"It's no bother, especially for a hero," she teased.

"I thought perhaps we could have an early brunch, and then, if you'd like, we could take Katie back to school, let you see the place. It's really quite something—they even have tour groups going through, buying stuff from the craft shop."

Clint exhaled. "I'm sorry, but my time's all booked up. I'm going to New York for a couple of days, on business and also to see friends. So maybe I can have a raincheck?" He smiled down at Katie.

Although he spoke warmly, Regina probed beneath the surface with a pang of sadness. He'd let his guard down last night, but it was back up today. She glanced at him, then Katie, and lowered her head. *I pushed too hard,* she thought, her eyelids prickling. *I got greedy, wanting too much.*

Blinking, she looked up with a steady smile. "Okay, one raincheck, good for a month of Sundays," she said lightly.

"Thank you. I'll grab a bite later. So if you'll excuse me, I'll go pack."

Regina's eyes flashed cold fire. "And if you'll excuse me, am I permitted to ask when you'll be back? I don't know the rules here, Clint."

Clint stared at her, rattled as much by her coolness as her question. "I didn't know we had any rules," he said, openly puzzled. "I certainly haven't made any." He ran a hand through his damp hair. "Do you want rules, Regina?"

"I— No, I guess not." Regina hesitated; was it a lady friend he was seeing in New York? Just the possibility was infuriating. "Just a minute," she said, glancing at Katie.

Taking his hand, Regina led him into the kitchen. "No, that's not true. There are rules. Fundamental rules, in my opinion. I don't sleep around. And I certainly don't sleep with men who have more than one bed partner at a time. If I'm it, then *that's* it. If you want to play musical beds, count me out.''

Clint swore under his breath. ''I thought that was a given. I don't play musical beds, Regina. In fact, I haven't been to bed with a woman in.... I don't know how many months, but I do know it's been a long time. Until you.''

Why me? The question almost slipped past her tongue. Silencing it, Regina expelled a shaky breath. ''Okay, then. It's a monogamous relationship. The only other rule is simple consideration.''

Acting on impulse, she caught his face and kissed him, hot and hard and forever.

Clint gripped her shoulders, holding her pressed against him for a time out of time while his head swam and his heart thundered, and he desperately needed air. But to break the delicious connection was a crazy idea. He had to have more and more....

Pulling away, Regina sighed against his chest where her head lay like some bright flower. Breathing hard, Clint struggled to regain control, and found he really didn't want it. Only when she stepped back and smiled at him did he make an effort.

''I'll be back Wednesday evening,'' he said gruffly.

''Okay. Well, I better get Katie ready to go,'' Regina said. ''Have a good time in New York, Clint.''

When she finally remembered to check on the biscuits, they were burned to a crisp.

Clad in a pin-striped suit tailored for him in London, wearing handsome ostrich-skin boots and carrying his intriguingly battered Stetson, Clint Whitfield strode through the crowded New York restaurant with an insouciant air of confidence. Whether on the tawny plains of Africa, the misty boulevards of Paris or here in the marbled splendor of a New York skyscraper, he possessed the ability to slip effortlessly into the prevailing milieu. Like a lion in tall grass, he thought, dry humored. Everyone just assumed he was part of it.

It had been his late wife who had provided egress into the upper echelons of society. She'd taken a rawboned lad fresh out of vet school, and had polished the rough diamond only she could see, until it was fit to wear on her arm.

She was still opening doors for him, he mused, pausing to put on his hat, the brim low and angled. He paid no attention to the glances of elegant women seated at equally elegant tables. As he left the restaurant, his attention was turned inward, to a misty memory of the week he and Barbara had spent in New York celebrating their fifth anniversary.

First-class all the way, he recalled. The first time he'd experienced such luxury. And he'd paid for every cent of it. Otherwise, there would have been no trip, no celebration, he admitted, stepping out the door into cool, hazy sunlight. His stiff-necked pride wouldn't have permitted it.

He chuckled. *Stiff-necked pride;* her description, spoken teasingly, eyes twinkling as she rebuked him. A thread of seriousness there, he reflected, still caught in the past's hazy web. He'd been too uptight about her money. If only he could have realized then what he knew now, that it wasn't money that counted.

Sometimes he wondered what he'd ever done to deserve the love of such a splendid woman. The best thing was being able to remember her in this soft, tender light. Any residue of bitterness was his own doing.

He wondered, too, without naming names, if another woman could understand his feelings and accept them without pain or censure. Would she, if not now, then later come to resent the enduring power of the past? He wasn't an accomplished liar, so pretending was out of the question....

The blare of a taxi's horn jolted him back to the present. Flustered, he paused at the curb. Since he had several hours to kill before his return flight to Houston, he opted to walk the ten blocks to his hotel. He needed the exercise. Besides, he'd get there much faster than those poor souls waiting out traffic jams, he thought ironically. The impatience burning inside him like a living flame would not tolerate that kind of delay.

He'd never felt so eager to get back, to anywhere. Instantly his mind responded to that admission by flying to the cause with a blast of mental fanfare. *Regina.* Her name added kindling to the fire, conjuring up as it did images so sweet and sexy he thought he might combust right here on Park Avenue. He disliked feeling so needful. But he didn't know how to stop it, and that gave him an alarming sensation of careening out of control.

By the time he was on the plane bound for home, Clint felt two sizes too big for his skin. He was finding it harder and harder to close himself off from Regina's invasive charm. It was bad enough that he was starting to care for her—it would be sheer idiocy to even consider caring for a special-needs child. *I loved once, and look what it cost me,* he reflected, accepting a glass of wine from the flight attendant. He wouldn't risk loving again.

But he didn't know how to stop that, either.

Then there were Regina's rules to deal with. He truly hadn't thought of burdening their relationship with rules. It simply wasn't serious enough—weren't they in accord on that? Or maybe he was reading something entirely different into what he'd thought of as mutual pleasure.

Giving and getting, deriving comfort from intimacy, enjoying the friendship that had sprung up between them; this did not require binding rules.

Oh, doesn't it? he mocked his arbitrary decision. *What if she wanted to see someone besides you?*

Clint stared out the window, seeing not clouds, but Regina's face, laughing, crying, sleeping. So vulnerable. A tidal wave of tenderness broke over him, making him catch his breath with its force. And he wondered again, perturbed again, no answer, again; what was he going to do about Regina Flynn?

What was she going to do about Clint Whitfield? Regina mused as she walked through the soft October dusk. She knew he'd be returning to Kenya in a week or two; he'd been very clear about that. And fair, she conceded. He'd made sure she knew from the start that their relationship was temporary. So she couldn't say she'd been misled, now or in the future.

Despite her staunch resolve, forcing herself to face facts was especially hard where he was concerned. It was so pleasant just to drift along on a cloud of illusion, pretending this was her house and that when she unlocked the door, there'd be light and warmth, sounds of music mingling with Katie's joyous lilt, children's voices—two, perhaps three—and overriding it all, Clint's husky laughter....

"Dream on, Regina," she grumbled, hurrying through the cool, quiet foyer. The only sounds were a chiming clock, and the tap-tap-tap of her heels on the marble floor, a peculiarly lonely sound. The sound of oneness, she thought, turning on another lamp.

When the house blazed with light, the aura of loneliness faded somewhat. Smiling at the lush purple blooms on her African violet, Regina opened her briefcase and took out the memo from Lamar.

He'd offered her the Dallas office. Taken by surprise, she had thanked him, and said she needed time to think it over.

Another decision to make, she mused, scanning the lines that would change her life again, were she to accept this lateral move in her career. She shook her head. Not that she wasn't tempted—there was a nice raise in salary with the new position—but Dallas was too far from Katie's school.

"End of debate," she said, her firm tone belying the wistfulness in her gaze. She wasn't a martyr, heavens no! But sometimes a tinge of regret did slip into decisions she'd had to make over the years.

She wondered if Clint would understand and agree with her decisions, or if, manlike, he'd have totally different priorities. Probably so.

You can't stay and I can't go.

Her own voice tugged painfully at her heartstrings. Another resolute, no-nonsense judgment she'd made without flinching. But this one, deliberately crushing her implausible new dream, would hurt far past tomorrow's promise.

Maybe I could change his mind about leaving.

Regina's chin jerked up as the sly thought slipped into her mind. She honestly hadn't tried to bind him with feminine wiles. In fact, she didn't quite know how to work up a good case of wiles. She'd never been a flirty, head-tossing, eye-batting female and had no desire to start now.

So pull back, Regina, put up some defensive walls, she advised herself. And you know what to do about Clint Whitfield. You're going to cool it.

She stuck a frozen entree into the microwave and poured a glass of milk. Minutes later, her mouth curled as she caught sight of herself in a mirror, peeling away the tinfoil on a steaming packet of macaroni and cheese.

Lifting her glass of milk, she toasted her image with a hollow laugh; just another evening at home with Regina Flynn.

At that moment she had no idea what she'd do or say if Clint walked into the kitchen. So much for self-discipline.

But the macaroni and cheese were surprisingly good.

Nine

Clint drove home with only one thought in mind—
just getting there. Leaving La Guardia Airport, his
plane had been delayed for two hours, sitting on the
runway with a full load of irate passengers. His Kenyan experience, lying in wait for an animal to be
tagged for tracking purposes, had taught him how to
wait without angst.

Another trick was to relax, close his eyes and permit
his mind to unreel a stream of mental images. *Morn-
ings on the Serengeti, sunlight on dew-wet grasses,
tawny hills undulating against a pure blue sky. Nights
spent under that same sky now black velvet, spangled
with countless stars, so brilliant he'd felt he could
gather them like diamonds strewn down some ancient
river bed.*

*The animals—long-necked giraffes; sleek zebras;
suspicious rhinos; ambling elephants, ears flapping,*

afraid of nothing. Lions, hippos, cheetahs; like God, he loved them all.

And don't forget the butchers, he would remind himself when he needed a gritty touch of reality. Coming upon magnificent animals slaughtered for their horns or tusks had filled him with fury and loathing. Poachers, he'd stated grimly, deserved to suffer a similar fate. Mostly though, they were arrested and carted off to jail by increasingly zealous rangers.

By replaying scenes from his African sojourn, he could while away the hours regardless of where he happened to be. Still, on a plane bound for Houston, he'd been hard put to control his frustration. By the time they landed at Bush Airport, his nerves were badly frayed.

As he wheeled into his driveway, his mind focused on Regina Flynn, an irritant, he thought moodily, much like a grain of sand inside an oyster. It was after ten. Would she still be up? If she was, would she welcome him home? And if she wasn't up, would she welcome him to her bed?

His gnawing questions were also irritating. He'd made some resolutions while in New York. Being away from her, walking the streets of a busy, bustling city that never slept, had lent an odd clarity to their relationship. Cut it down to size, he thought. But the nearer he'd come to home, the more he'd realized nothing had changed. He was seething with the same impatient eagerness that marked his last out-of-town trip.

He parked in the circular driveway, his breath stealing out in a long sigh. The lights were on, a welcome-home symbol that squeezed his heart. Her car must be parked in the space he'd finally cleared in the garage.

When he stood in the foyer, testing the air like an

animal just emerging from hibernation, the silence brought him down to earth. He tossed his hat on the desk and walked on to his bedroom. He was *not* going to listen at her door. But his body overruled his mind. For an electric moment he ceased to breathe, his entire being on hold, listening so hard his ears crackled.

His broad shoulders slumped. Disappointment, abrasively keen, propelled him on down the hall to his own room. He undressed by rote, tossed clothing into the hamper, stepped under the stinging needles of a hot shower with a gusty sigh. Bowing his head, he let the water beat on his stiff neck muscles, while he planned his next move.

Not much to plan, he thought sourly. Towel off, put on silk boxer shorts, a robe and house slippers. When he'd done that, he sauntered to the kitchen, his heart still hoping she'd be there. But she wasn't, and when he checked, he saw that the garage was devoid of her little blue car.

Fool! he castigated himself, slamming the door shut. Watch what you wish for—you might get it! In no mood to analyze that thought, he poured a glass of milk and sat down at the counter.

The silence of an empty house beat like a tom-tom in his ears. *Exactly as it had done the first night he'd spent, alone and sleepless, in his jewel of a new home,* he reflected. A cruel farce played by sadistic gods? Or just the luck of the draw?

Stymied by his enigmatic train of thought, he folded his arms on the counter and laid down his head, to wait out the silence.

At ten-thirty, Regina, laden down with her brief-case, a shopping bag and several plastic grocery bags, cast a joyous glance at Clint's truck before hurrying into the house. She set everything down on the foyer floor and called his name.

"Well, here you are!" he said, appearing in the arched doorway like the first of a genie's three wishes.

Regina smiled because she had to. Her heart was turning cartwheels. Very hard to breathe when your heart is romping through a field of daisies, she thought with puckish humor.

"Hi, Clint." She slipped off her shoulder bag, desperately battling the urge to throw herself into his arms. With lithe, graceful movements, she leaned against the doorway, bent her leg and pulled off one pump, then the other. She straightened, the black patent pumps dangling from two fingers. His face was expressionless, but those sky-blue eyes followed her every move, she noticed.

She smiled brightly. "So how was your trip?"

"My trip was fine," Clint said.

His annoyance swelled like a balloon when he looked at her. That coolness in her eyes, that elusive little smile—damn! And the way she tossed her head—double damn!

He gathered the grocery bags and carried them to the counter.

"Working late?"

"Yep. Then I went shopping. For Katie." Dropping her pumps, she took off her jacket and hung it over a chair. "She's very hard on shoes—loses a pair a week! So how was your trip?" Red-tipped fingers flew to her mouth. "Oh, I already asked you that."

"And I answered." Clint's gaze was riveted on her scarlet lips. She really did have the most captivating mouth—little peaks on the upper lip, a full, round bottom.

Lip, bottom *lip,* he stressed to his lusty inner self. Although her bottom, in that fitted skirt, was definitely full and round.

The thought aroused him. As if I needed help in that department, he thought wryly. His gaze refocused as she began unloading groceries. She reached up and down, bending to put refrigerator foods in the crisper, straightening to reach the spice rack, stretching across the counter to refill the fruit bowl, altogether creating a ravishing picture of femininity. Her demure white blouse with its Peter Pan collar only enhanced her appeal.

"What have you been up to since I left?" he asked lightly.

"Not much. Working, at the office and at home on my laptop, talking with Katie…" She brushed back curls that had escaped their combs. "Having dinner with clients."

"What clients?" Clint leaned against the counter. "I didn't know you had to do that."

"Well, it's my choice. I mean, I'm not pressured into it or anything like that. But sometimes it's an enjoyable task. You should be able to relate to that," she added with a sidelong glance.

"I guess I should." Clint's jaw hardened as a surge of unreasoning emotion swept through him. Jealousy? *Don't be ridiculous,* he berated his knowing inner voice. "But mine is always strictly business," he stated.

"That's good. If you can keep it that way." Ignoring his quick stir, she continued, "I'm going to shower. If you're hungry, there's lunch meat in the fridge.''

Regina closed her bathroom door with a hissing breath of relief. She had to lean against its solid surface because her legs were trembling. She was so glad to see him! A gladness that touched the sublime, she thought. Her entire body was aflame with desire. Just imagining him touching her here…and here…. She shivered.

With quickening eagerness, she undressed and showered, toweled off, sprayed the air with an orange-blossom scent and stepped into its fragrant mist. Was it too strong? She waved the air with both hands, but the mist had settled, so there was nothing to be done other than take another shower. ''Heck with that,'' she muttered.

Pulling on her favorite drawstring pajamas of soft white cotton, she brushed out her hair and swept it atop her head, tied with an apple-green ribbon. It wouldn't stay tied for long, she thought with a secretive little smile.

Satin scuffs silenced her footsteps as she returned to the great room. Her gaze lost no time locating Clint. He stood before an open French door, his dark head bowed as if in thought.

Or in memory, she amended with a pinch of hurt. She didn't resent his memories, for that would be stupid. But she'd like to share them. So far, he hadn't responded to that extent. Maybe he never would. Maybe his secretiveness was a vital defense. At least to him it was. To her, it was frustration.

She walked on to the kitchen and opened the refrigerator. ''I made fruit salad, if you'd like some.''

''No, thank you.''

She shrugged, indifferent, or so it seemed to Clint. His anger flared to something like a briar-patch suit, itching and stinging and just generally driving him mad. Meeting her ice-green gaze was the last straw. The welter of confused emotions made his head swim in a most disagreeable way, and if he had time to think, he'd realize he'd never felt anything like it before.

Actually one part of him did recognize that, but the rest of him was filling up with masculine pride, and he reacted with lusty pleasure.

"I missed you," he said, his long strides taking him to the kitchen too fast to dwell on the intimacy his words implied.

She stepped back from him.

"Regina, I drove home on fire with the thought of seeing you again," he continued hoarsely. "Holding you again, loving you again—"

"You mean having sex with me again." Regina eeled out of reach. "Which isn't a put-down. The sex is great. But let's call it what it is."

Smoldering blue eyes narrowed to a squint. "And what is that?"

She faced him, chin up, eyes gleaming with feminine challenge. The soft cotton fabric clung to her breasts; a hint of taut nipples added to her saucy defiance. "I just told you. Sex. Good sex. Great sex. Sublime sex, even. But still, just sex." She turned her back to him. "And I haven't decided if I'm in the mood yet."

Stung as if by a thousand hornets, Clint grasped her shoulders and drew her back against him while he tried to formulate a sensible reply. But he didn't have time to form even a verb, much less an entire sentence. He

groaned as she squirmed against his clasp. "Stop..."
He caught his breath. "Regina, stop that!"

"Let me go!" she ordered imperiously. Exhilarated
by this thrilling duel of wills, she raised her voice to
a royal command. "Clint, I am warning you, let me
go."

"You really want me to let you go?" he asked huskily. "If you do, I will."

"No! Yes! I do!" she sputtered.

Instantly his arms encircled her midriff, locking her
snug into his embrace, which absolutely infuriated Regina—she liked it too much!

"Damn you, Clint Whitfield!" she gritted, twisting
around to face him. An electric excitement sizzled in
the meeting of bodies. She pushed at his chest with an
outraged hiss. "Let go of me, you big *oaf!*"

Incredibly conflicted, Clint gazed down into sparkling green eyes. "I resent being called an oaf, Gina,"
he warned, laughter creeping into his voice as he
watched her furious face.

"I don't give a big fat fig what you resent—take
your hands off me, I said!" Regina demanded. It was
lovely being a captive in his brawny arms. And he'd
called her Gina again. *Like tenderness given a voice,*
she thought. "Macho male," she muttered, flashing
him a look.

The laughter Clint restrained exploded in a burst of
fiery excitement as she twisted in his arms. He trapped
her face with his and kissed her, his taut body trembling with the passion she ignited. The shock of holding a tempestuous little wildcat instead of the steady,
common-sense Regina, was stunningly erotic.

The lovely wildling still pushed at him, still challenging his power to tame her, even while her lips drew him in with a torrid kiss.

His arms tightened, fusing her enchanting body to his. In a flash her fury changed to an equally ardent passion, one that threatened to consume him. Clint scooped her up and carried her to her bedroom.

He let her slide slowly down his body, savoring every inch of her descent, until her feet touched the carpet. She lifted her face, a Mona Lisa smile seducing his gaze. He took the ribbon from her hair and let it fall in satiny curls around his wrists.

She in turn helped him remove his robe. Her fingers slipped under the waistband of his shorts and down his hips in maddening caress, while her lips created another erotic path from his chin to his navel. When she withdrew her fingers and stepped back from him, Clint clumsily undressed.

The bed was unmade and her tangled sheets were fragrant with the scent of Gina, an aphrodisiac in itself, he thought. He stretched out on her perfumed bower with its flowered linens and deep rose comforter, to wait in hot anticipation.

Taking her time, Regina peeled off her pajamas, standing, for an electrifying instant, clad only in a tiny wedge of white satin attached to the thin waistband encircling her hips. Then, with two fingers, she pulled the sensuous garment down her legs and kicked it off her bare feet.

Regina heard his sharp intake of breath. Smiling to herself, she stood beside the bed, a hand on one hip, the other hand between her breasts. Maybe I do know a wile or two, she thought, feeling the potent effect of feminine power.

Her smile tantalizing, secretive, she met his gaze in

a wordless message. He must have understood it; with a ferocious growl, her caveman grabbed her hips and pulled her down atop him.

She lay quiet for a moment, savoring the stimulating sensation of having a very masculine man cushioning her body. Then, wanting to know all of him, she slipped through his arms. When he came up on one elbow, she pushed him right back down. "My turn to look," she murmured.

While Clint lay quiescent, she explored his body as thoroughly as he had hers. Her fingers probed his chest, stroking the hard male nipples, delighting in the texture of the dark, springy hair arrowing down his flat stomach...

She bade him turn over, and when he obeyed, she traced the lines of his back all the way to his heels and up again.

His body quivered under those tantalizing fingers. Her caresses were delicious pleasure, but Clint could only bear so much. With a husky laugh, he flipped her over on her back and lowered himself down upon her intoxicating softness.

Despite the rage of heat in his groin, it was a sweet, euphoric coupling. To Clint's surprise, he felt no frenzied urge to end it, no need to move roughly or in haste. Just lying here, feeling himself inside her, was as pleasing as the wildest sexual gymnastics. He kissed her flushed face, tasting it, delighting in knowing her features by taste alone.

"Oh, this is wonderful."

"Yes." Her lips brushed his. "Yes."

He tasted her tongue, then pushed his own into the honeyed cave of her mouth. How soft, how delicious her mouth was! Drawing back, he smiled at her. In defense, she lowered her gaze until only a sliver of green shown through her thick lashes.

It went on and on, this curiously sweet, gentle coupling....

And then they were caught in a rich, hot spiral of mind-spinning excitement...flung heavenward on a wave of explosive ecstasy...and left to drift slowly down to earth again....

Lying on his side, his head pillowed on her shoulder, Clint closed his eyes to better experience the sense of bliss that had settled around them in the softly lit bedroom. Drowsily he kissed her cheek—and tasted tears.

Startled, he rolled onto his stomach in order to see her face. Crystal teardrops bejeweled her dark lashes and ran in tiny rivulets down her temples.

"Oh, no," he said on a trailing sigh. "Did I hurt you?"

"No, no." Her eyes opened, wet and shining. "It was just so wonderful, so..." She shook her head. "It was magical, Clint. You may find that word amusing, but to me, it was that and more."

"I don't find it amusing. In fact, I agree."

Instantly regretting his testy tone, Clint kissed away her tears, then turned on his back, bringing her with him until her head rested on his chest. "Your arms are cold," he scolded, drawing the comforter over them.

For the moment Regina was silent. The joy coursing through her could not be expressed in mere words. She wanted to hold on to this moment, this fragile element of nontime, as long as possible. Her need now was for verbal intimacy. But how to start without raising his guard again?

"How many times have you been in love?" she asked, yawning.

"Once."

"But in high school, and college?"

"Crushes. Infatuation. Simple lust. But my wife… That's love. The real thing. I have no doubt that we'd have grown old together if we'd had the chance."

"I think it's wonderful that two people can form such a beautiful bond. I'm also awed that you can love so much, so deeply. In my opinion, finding that kind of love is as rare as finding a unicorn," she ended with a nervous little laugh.

"I don't know much about unicorns," he drawled. "Aren't they extinct?"

He's teasing me. Wonderful! "I think there still may be some around, in high, secret places, where the snow is so pure and white, it shields them from all eyes…." She laughed again. "Sorry. Got carried away there!"

She snuggled closer. Absently he stroked her hair.

"This fellow you were engaged to—did you love him?" Clint asked, his tone still disputing serious interest.

"I don't know. I thought I did, at the time. But in hindsight, I wonder. Maybe I was just needy—after all, Mom was gone and I was left with Katie. Maybe I just wanted someone to be with, because I was terrified of going it alone."

She sighed. "I still don't know. But it did hurt, being left at the altar, so to speak. It was a time of confusion and fear, rejection, anger, knowing he didn't care enough about me…."

"A bad time."

"A bad time," she echoed. "But we came through

it, and now I figure Katie and I can handle just about anything.''

The proud lilt in her voice drove a fist into Clint's midsection. She lay nestled in his arms, vulnerable, trusting, hanging on to his every word.

Oh, damn, he thought, what have I done?

Let her get too close, that's what, his sense of honor responded. *Why didn't you protect this lovely lady by keeping your distance? Dammit, it was supposed to be "hands off," remember? And while we're at it, why didn't you protect yourself?*

''Excuse me, I didn't hear what you said,'' Clint said apologetically. He'd heard her voice, but that was all.

''I said, you must really love working in Africa.''

''Yes, I do. It still has magic, even with so much destruction from the so-called civilized world. The Serengeti is one of the last remaining wildlife sanctuaries on earth. The very name translates from the Masai language to 'endless plains.' And they do appear endless, although of course they're not.''

He sighed and curved his other arm around her waist. ''Do you really want to hear this?''

''Oh, yes, I do!'' She snuggled closer. ''You have a gift for description, Clint, makes a person *see* what you're saying. Please, go on.''

Absurdly pleased by her praise, Clint felt the urge to shrug. Instead, he continued reflectively, ''The area is beautiful of itself, but add the animals, and it becomes a spectacle too majestic to even try to describe. Thousands of wildebeest flowing over the crest of a hill like some dark river, elephant families making their slow, plodding way to the watering holes, supremely top-of-the-food-chain, and yet, they're on the

endangered-species list. Because of man's greed for
money. Elephants really are caring, loving creatures.
They tend their children, protect their mates. My
friend has a small plane, a necessity, really, with such
vast distances. I'm also a pilot and sometimes I'd fly
alone, circling low enough to have a front-row seat to
this exhilarating marvel…."

Regina listened, entranced as his deep voice painted
pictures from his heart. When at last he fell silent, she
sighed, wishing she had something interesting to tell
him. Something that would keep him talking.

"I'm not surprised that you can fly a plane. With
all your talents? I'd be surprised if you didn't!" she
said, chuckling.

He looked abashed. "My folks gave me flying les-
sons as a graduation gift and I discovered I liked it."
He turned on his side and began playing with her hair.
"So what's new with you?" he asked lazily.

"Lamar offered me a position in Dallas." She snuggled her cheek into the path of his caressing fingers.
"A lateral move, I think it's called, but at least it implies that I'm back in his good graces."

Dallas. Bemused by his own puzzling feelings about
the offer, it took Clint a moment to respond. "So are
you going to accept it? It's not exactly a step up. And
why should you have to get back in his good graces?"

"Clint, you know why—"

"No. No, dammit, I don't. I told the agency that
everything was all right—I made it crystal-clear that I
appreciated my house sitter's excellent services. Lamar has no reason to run end games around you!"

"I'm not sure what that means, but I like it," she
replied with a soft laugh. "Anyway, I'll tell him tomorrow that I'm not accepting the position. Which

may count as another strike against me— I've already turned down a move to Austin.'' She sighed. ''I really regretted that one. I think I'd love living in the Hill Country. But I have to remain in this area, and that's that.''

''Well, if he gives you any more trouble...''

''If he does,'' she agreed to the tacit offer of help. Feeling protected was wonderfully sweet. She curled a leg over his, enjoying the intimacy of casual touch. ''I'm picking up Katie Saturday and we're going to the zoo. You're welcome to join us if you'd like.''

Clint's breath tangled as he remembered Katie's small hand slipping into his, her lovely eyes sparkling with the simple joy of being alive on such a beautiful day.

''The zoo. You know, I used to hate those things,'' he mused. ''Even as a boy, I was appalled that an animal as magnificent as a tiger or a lion was doomed to pace a concrete floor in a wire pen. I thought it barbaric that any animal should live out its life caged up for the entertainment of kids like me. They should be living in the wilds, like nature intended.''

He dropped a kiss on her hair. ''Now, though, weird as it seems, zoos and the wilds have reversed roles. It's the zoos that are saving endangered species from extinction. Remember that baby panda born in the San Diego Zoo?''

''Yes, I do remember that!'' Regina exclaimed. ''They put it on the Internet so people could follow the baby's every move.''

''Well, sadly enough, all that hype was merited. Pandas don't like to reproduce in captivity. There's a hundred or so in zoos worldwide, and barely a thousand in the wilds of Asia. Their habitat keeps shrinking and no one gives a damn,'' he ended on a note of bitterness.

"Someone does give a damn,'' she said softly. "You do. And I think what you're doing, raising money to preserve these innocent victims of progress, is just short of noble.''

Beautifully embarrassed, Clint responded with a short laugh. "I doubt that last part,'' he said drily. "Tell me, what caused Katie's handicap? Was she born that way?''

"Yes and no. She was perfect up until the time she was born. I was there with Mom—Dad was off on a business trip—and when I saw our baby, my heart just about broke. She was a 'blue baby,' deprived of oxygen too long during the birth process. We didn't know how much damage she suffered, some, of course...but you can't kill hope, regardless of how unlikely the outcome.''

Regina turned her face up to his. "You've seen her, you know how marvelous she is. You just take that and build on it as far as you can.''

"You're far more resilient than I'll ever be,'' he said heavily. Rolling away from her, he got up and put on his shorts. He had to get out of this lovely bedroom with its far too lovely occupant. Something was building inside him, something alarming, because it threatened to shred his control.

"I'm not sleepy yet,'' he said, meeting her puzzled gaze. "You get some sleep, though. I'll just go catch up on the news.''

Giving her no time to protest, he grabbed his robe and walked out the door.

Regina sunk back down on her pillow, her eyes smarting. Since he hadn't responded to her zoo invitation, she could only assume that he didn't wish to go with her and Katie.

Not too surprising, she chided her teary self. Men just didn't want to get involved, a lesson she'd learned the hard way.

Well, that was okay. She'd already reconciled herself to going it alone.

"But that doesn't mean I don't dream of having a mate," she whispered. Not just any mate, though. Eyes tightly shut, she looked inward and faced a frightening truth. She loved Clint Whitfield, loved him deeply, intensely, joyously. "Terrifyingly," she added, pulling the covers up to her chin.

She had no doubts as to how she felt about him. For her, the wisdom of loving him was what was in question.

Wise or not, she loved him. "So there's no use angsting about it," Regina chided the anxiety swirling around her admission.

One could always hope.

Ten

When Regina awoke the next morning, her bedside lamp had been turned off and the comforter pulled up around her shoulders. As realization set in, her eyes filled with tears. For the first time in years, someone had tucked her in.

Oh, Clint! As she bathed and dressed, little puffs of happiness kept interfering. She had to redo her mascara twice. But at last she was ready for work. She stepped into her pumps, adjusted her dove-gray suit and soft blue blouse, and headed for the kitchen.

The fragrance of fresh coffee was all that greeted her. Disappointed, she lingered over breakfast, waiting for Clint to make an appearance. She wondered why he had gone back to his own bed last night. Any number of things could have prevented his return, she reasoned. "Including my invitation to accompany Katie and me to the zoo," she admitted.

That stung. She wanted to think he wasn't avoiding another encounter with her beloved sister. But since he hadn't even mentioned it...

"You keep on leading with your heart, Gina, and someone's going to break it one of these days," she concluded. Her feelings for Clint were proof that she'd never loved before. So this was a whole new ball game, and she had no idea how to play.

Her head snapped up at the sound of footsteps coming down the hall. Her pulses scrambled as she beheld him, tall, dark and charismatic in a black shirt and cords. She greeted him with a breathless "Good morning! Did you sleep well?"

"Well enough." He paused. "A lot better if I'd slept with you."

Regina laughed. "Well, you were welcome to." She ran a caressing finger down the faint white line of the scar on his cheek. "Coffee?" she asked.

He nodded and she poured for him. Another small pleasure, she thought. She delighted in doing for him. She set the mug on a folded cloth napkin and handed it to him, with love, although he wasn't aware of it.

"Thanks." Distractedly he sipped the hot, black brew. "Listen, about last night..." His gaze met hers squarely. "I didn't get around to replying to your question about accompanying you and Katie to the zoo."

Awkwardness suddenly entered the warm atmosphere. Hating it, Regina said in a rush, "Oh, that's all right, Clint. Really, it is. I shouldn't have asked you to do that again."

His brows drew together. "Do what again?"

"Go somewhere with Katie and me. I shouldn't have tried to fob her off on you again— I knew you weren't comfortable around her. So let's table this discussion before it gets any more unwieldy.''

Clint gazed into his coffee cup. There had been no belligerence, no accusation in her soft voice. "You're wrong about my reaction to Katie. The only reason I passed on the zoo trip was because…'' His gaze raised to connect with her watchful green eyes.

"Because?'' she prompted softly.

"Because she damn near breaks my heart!'' he burst out.

Regina's hands flew to her chest as she stared at him. *Don't gush,* she warned herself. "Oh, Clint, that's so sweet! And you're right. She's both a joy and a heartache to me, too.'' She heard herself gushing. Reining in her delight, she steadied her voice. "I'm so glad to know your reason for avoiding her. I—I wondered if maybe you didn't like her.''

"Oh, for God's sake, Regina, she's a sweetheart. You know that,'' he said gruffly. He slid onto a stool. "Anyway, I'll be heading toward Amarillo this weekend.''

"You're going to see your parents!''

Clint smiled briefly. "Yes. About time, I guess.''

"I guess.'' Had he finally realized the importance of family? Trying to shush her singing heart, Regina put two slices of bread in the toaster. "Clint, I've been thinking… Those boxes in the garage—couldn't I help you unpack and put away the contents?''

Clint didn't answer for a long thirty seconds. "No, there's nothing in those boxes I need. They're things like books, pictures, china, silver…. Nothing important.''

"I think they're very important,'' she retorted. "To a woman, anyway. I don't understand why…'' She hesitated, afraid of overstepping. "Well, I can't see moving into this beautiful house and then just leaving the pretty things boxed up. Didn't your wife have time to put them away?"

"No." Clint stood up. "My wife never had a chance to put them away, because she never had a chance to live in this 'beautiful house.'"

Regina's mouth fell open. "She never lived here? But I thought…"

"You thought wrong. I could never have made love to another woman in this house with memories of her living here."

Regina looked away. Sensing her hurt, Clint blew out a hard breath. "If I'm being too blunt—"

"No! No, you're not. Sometimes the truth sounds hard just because it *is* true. I respect your…consideration, I guess you could call it. I mean, I know what you mean," she said with a tiny laugh, "which isn't to say I'm making sense. Please, go on."

"You're making sense. Anyway, the house wasn't finished yet," he continued matter-of-factly. "As usual, hardheaded me refused to move in until every last nail was in place. We had only another month or so to wait, as it turned out."

He roughed up his hair. "After—afterward, I went ahead and finished the house, I guess to honor all the energy and ardor she put into it. I even sold our condo, thinking I could make it here. But I couldn't. So it was off to Kenya and end of story."

Regina cleared the lump in her throat. "That beautiful rose garden?"

"Hers. Created by the landscape firm that did the rest of the grounds. She chose the roses, agonizing over each selection. After they started blooming, she'd come over every chance she got and deadhead, weed, cut armfuls of her favorites...'' Clint sat down again, his back to the counter.

Regina struggled with a fierce urge to hold him. He wouldn't want it, she suspected. Wishing she had time to go over everything he'd said, she touched his shoulder.

"Clint, I'm sorry. Once again I've stuck my nose in where it had no right to be. But I do thank you for talking so freely with me." She checked her watch and sighed. "Well, it's time for me to go to work. When will you be leaving?"

"Today, I think. I have a luncheon date, then I'll head out. There's a few friends I want to look up while I'm in the area. I don't know when I'll be back," he said sincerely. "It's sort of a play-it-by-ear thing."

"Okay. By the way, thanks for tucking me in last night. It's been a long time since someone's done that. Your toast has popped up. Bye." Standing on tiptoe, she kissed his mouth, her heart jumping when his arms swirled around her in a tight embrace.

"I'll miss you," she said when she could.

"That's nice," he replied, kissing the tip of her nose. "You take care, now."

"You, too." Wondering at the identity of his luncheon date, Regina ruffled his hair, then grabbed her bag and briefcase, and hurried to the door.

He didn't stop her. Of course she couldn't stay, but it would have been nice if he'd tried.

Saturday morning Regina picked up Katie and they lunched at a place that had terrible pizza, but wondrous video games. With half her mind on her sister and the other half on Clint, Regina found time drawing out like pulled taffy.

When they finally arrived at the house, Katie wanted to swim. Agreeably, having heated the pool beforehand, Regina laid out their bathing suits.

The water, though tepid, still felt chilly to Regina. But Katie found it delightful and had no intention of coming out during daylight hours. Laughing at her antics, Regina exited the pool to answer the intercom's buzz.

"Yes, who is it?" she asked.

"Kathryn Brandt."

Caught off guard, Regina stammered, "Oh, my. Mrs. B-Brandt—"

"Kathryn."

"Kathryn," she echoed. "Clint isn't here, and I can't answer the door because I have a child in the pool. She can't swim, so I—I can't leave her alone in the water." She gave a quick, nervous laugh. "And there's no way I'm going to get her out of there right now!"

"That's all right, my dear. I'll just come in the side gate. It's unlocked, isn't it?"

"No. But I can run up and unlock it. Won't take a sec." Warning Katie to stay in the shallow water, Regina raced across the terrace to the gate, trying desperately to remember the code while keeping an eye on Katie. She fumbled with buttons, and miraculously the lock opened.

"Please, come in, Kathryn," she said with a sweeping gesture. "I have a pitcher of cold lemonade at poolside if you'd like."

She needn't have tried persuasion, Regina thought dryly; her guest was already en route to the pool.

"Well, hello," Kathryn said, stopping at the edge of the deck. "And who are you, sweetie?"

Katie dimpled.

"This is Katie, my young sister," Regina answered for her. "Katie, this is Kathryn Brandt."

Watching Kathryn interact with Katie, Regina inwardly sighed. *Lord, I wish Katie had grandparents. I also wish I had something on besides this faded old suit!* Kathryn looked exquisite in a black coatdress with large white buttons from throat to hem.

Every hair was in place, of course. Regina swiped at her own wayward curls. Apparently Katie had taken a liking to their visitor; she was chattering like a blue jay.

"Katie lives at her school during the week," Regina cut in. "I get her on weekends and we have lots of fun, don't we, love?"

"And what school is that?" Kathryn asked. When Regina told her, the older woman nodded. "I've often visited your school's shop, Katie. They make beautiful pottery—angels, garden statues, candleholders...." She smiled down at Katie. "Have I seen anything of yours?"

"No, she doesn't work in the pottery shed," Regina said, her limpid gaze on Katie's glowing face. "She's a gardener, works in the greenhouse transplanting seedlings into larger pots," she added in the same bright voice. She felt uncomfortable with the older woman.

"Well, maybe I've bought one of your plants," Kathryn said. "I do think I'll have that lemonade now." Sitting down, she kicked off her shoes and wriggled her toes luxuriously. "Shoes do pinch," she said, sighing. Her gaze slid over Regina, who was putting on a short terry robe. "You're very attractive, Regina. I can see why Clint has stayed around so long this time."

Regina blushed furiously. "I doubt I've held him here, Mrs.—uh, Kathryn. At any rate, he'll probably be returning to Kenya soon."

Kathryn Brandt nodded. "That's his way of coping, my dear. Only thing is, what is he running from this time?"

"The same thing as last time, I suspect. You know he isn't over your daughter's death, don't you?" Regina said bluntly.

"Well, they were so in love." Kathryn sipped lemonade, making a face at its tartness. "They had their differences, but that never shook their deep affection and regard for each other."

"I know," Regina said softly.

"Then you also know, or at least suspect, that he's trapped in the bitterness of his loss. There are many stages of grieving. He hasn't gotten past the anger and guilt stage. Holds himself to blame for everything."

Kathryn shook her sleek head. "I still grieve, too. After all, she was my daughter long before she became his wife. But my philosophy of life and death has helped me to move on."

"He rarely talks about her to me," Regina said. "Except to tell me how much he loves—*loved* her, although I suspect that *loves* is more precise."

"I don't agree. I think he uses *loves* like a fence around his heart." Kathryn set down her glass, her gaze on Katie, who sat on the steps splashing water. "To me, he's the son I never had. He's a good man...something that's also on the endangered list, if there's any truth to what I read in women's magazines and see on soap operas,'' she said with a faint smile.

Her gaze flitted to the butterfly hovering over Regina's garden. ''I had lunch with Caroline this week. Fascinating woman. A world traveler. Caroline's spending Thanksgiving in Nairobi.''

Feeling as if she'd been punched in the stomach and determined not to reveal it, Regina said lightly, ''That sounds lovely.'' *Is Clint planning to be in Nairobi for Thanksgiving?* ''I envy her, being able to travel wherever she wishes.''

Kathryn gave her a quizzical look. ''You can't?''

Regina glanced at Katie. ''No, I'm afraid I'm quite firmly tethered to my little spot of earth.''

Following Regina's gaze, Kathryn nodded. ''I see. Are your parents living?''

''No, it's just Katie and me.'' Regina poured herself a glass of lemonade. ''Kathryn…'' *Don't even think about it!* warned her inner voice. ''Katie and I are going to the zoo tomorrow before I take her home. We'd love to have you go with us.''

''And I'd love to come with you, if I didn't have a pressing engagement tomorrow afternoon. A friend's wedding,'' she explained. Her wry smile flashed again. ''Something I've been considering lately,'' she confided.

The two women shared a conspiratory laugh.

A short time later, Kathryn folded her used napkin and stood up. ''Well, I'd best get going, leave you to enjoy your time with Katie.'' She waved to the girl splashing in the pool. ''She's darling, Regina,'' she said softly.

''Thank you. I think so, too. I'm sorry you must leave. I've enjoyed your visit,'' Regina said. She

walked her guest to the gate, her gaze pensive as she
bid Kathryn Brandt goodbye.

I wonder what that was about, she mused, watching
the elegant matron disappear around the corner of the
house. *Did she come to see Clint, or me? And if me,
why?*

Regina relocked the gate. "Just casual conversation?" she wondered aloud. "Or was she alerting me
to Caroline's plans to spend Thanksgiving in Nairobi
with her very own tour guide? If so, what the devil
am I supposed to do about it?" she muttered seething-
ly.

Another question followed on the heels of that one.
How much time had Clint spent with the fascinating
Caroline?

He said I'd be the only one, Regina reminded herself. *A closed relationship, and I believed him.*

Maybe I was foolish to trust him....

*No. No, dammit, I'm not playing that game. He gave
me his word, just as I gave mine. I'm not going to
cheapen what we've shared with doubt and suspicion.*

Jamming her hands into her pockets, she walked
back to the pool. Kathryn's intent really didn't matter.
Regina had no claim on Clint, and thus, no power to
challenge anyone's plans.

Sunday evening, Clint returned home shortly after
Regina. He found her outside on the pool deck, tend-
ing her "garden."

"That one looks pretty far gone," he said, startling
her into a little jump. "Sorry. Didn't mean to sneak
up on you." His gaze roamed her lithe and lovely
figure. The white shorts she wore displayed her round
rump and long, tanned legs to finger-curling perfec-

tion. The breeze played in her hair, lifting a bright tress and placing it across her lips. He brushed it back.

Regina stood perfectly still until she felt certain that her knees would lock upon command. The tremor in her legs came out in her voice as she greeted him. "Yes, that tomato plant's compost material," she agreed. "Poor thing, sitting out here in the hot sun day after day. Just plumb worn out. But this one—" she gestured to a plant lush with foliage and fruit "—a jalapeño pepper, thrives in the very same conditions." Her lashes swept up, revealing a glint of mischief. "Very hot pepper. Do you like hot sauce?"

"I love it." He slipped his hands under her arms and lifted her over the pot and into his embrace.

Keenly aware that her body perfectly aligned with his, Regina gasped at the tantalizingly light contact. "This pot," she gamely continued, "contains herbs that I use often. Mint, oregano, basil, chives—oh!"

The rest of her sentence was lost in a long, deep kiss.

"It's getting late," Clint said, peering at the darkened bedroom windows. "You want to go get something to eat? For some reason I'm starved!"

His wicked grin evoked a frown from Regina. They were in his room this time. "I'm starving, too, but I know why. I think I've just been ravished. And no, I don't want to go get something to eat. You stop that!" She smacked the hand stealing under the covers. "I'll fix us something. Something light—you don't want a heavy meal this late."

She caught his marauding hand and held it to her cheek. "How about scrambled eggs and biscuits? And some of my special blueberry preserves."

"Please tell me you're *not* going to tell me you made those preserves from blueberries you picked yourself," he said, running a finger along her jawline.

"Well, I did. One summer evening I went to the blueberry farm and picked enough for six pints of jam. I'm not without talents, Clint."

"Oh, I know that," he murmured, his unruly fingers slipping under the sheet.

She blushed. "Clint, are you trying to start something?"

"Don't I wish!" He sighed. "Unfortunately I need a little recovery time," he said sadly.

Regina burst out laughing and nearly cut his recovery time in half. He pulled her on top of him and held her imprisoned in his strong arms. "You're a lusty wench, wench," he said huskily. "You want to do something fun?"

"Fun? I thought we were doing something fun." She propped up on her arms. "What do you have in mind?"

"Umm, I don't know.... You want to play some poker? A card game, Gina," he added, eyes twinkling.

"Poker?" she echoed.

"You don't know how?"

"Of course I know how, but...now?"

"Why not now? Keep us occupied while I recuperate."

Her eyes narrowed. "We're playing for money?"

"Is there any other way? Chips and cards are in the closet."

He bounded out of bed and fetched the necessities for a card game. And soon, to Regina's amazement, they sat cross-legged on the bed, playing poker, yet!

It was hilarious fun. She swore he cheated and he

threatened to frisk her for hidden aces. That they could laugh and play ridiculous games felt wonderful, Regina thought, throwing in her last chip.

"How much did I lose?" she asked, scowling at his irrepressible grin.

"Plenty. But I'll consider other means of payment besides currency."

"Scoundrel!" she muttered, eyes flashing. Listening to his laughter, she wished he'd let go with a real laugh, from the heart, from the belly—hearty, open mirth. When he caught her head and held her lips to his for a sweet interval, she forgot to wish and just enjoyed.

Eventually, dressed in her favorite silk kimono, she made it to the kitchen. Clint, barefoot and blue-jeaned, roamed around the great room like a restless puma, picking up magazines and setting them down, checking her pitiful video collection. "Somewhere in those boxes out there I have over six hundred videos," he informed her.

Regina took eggs and canned biscuits from the refrigerator. "Well, I know where mine are, should I want to watch one."

"Ha." Clint sat down at the bar. "So, tell me about your weekend."

"You first. Did your visit home make you feel good?"

"Yeah, it did," he said on a faint note of surprise that set him to roaming again. "I think Mom and Dad are about resigned to me not coming back there to live. And that I won't remarry, so there'll be no horde of grandchildren. Although Mom wasn't quite as resigned to the latter."

"Amazing, isn't it, how a woman keeps on hoping?'' Regina said, breaking eggs so skillfully he stopped to watch.

Clint didn't know how to respond to that. ''I'm thinking of going to San Francisco to visit my brother.''

Regina whipped eggs. ''Oh, your brother. I'd forgotten! You mentioned him once, but I guess it didn't stick. When are you going?''

''Tomorrow, I guess. I'll stay a few days, try to reestablish our brotherhood, so to speak. Make sure he knows I have no prejudice against alternative lifestyles. Mom doesn't, either, but Dad...''

Comprehending his meaning, Regina replied, ''It seems to be harder on fathers.''

''Yeah. But I think he's slowly coming around.'' Clint indulged in a long, limbering stretch. ''So, how was your weekend with Katie?''

''Great,'' Regina enthused. Something warm and pleasing bound them together and she loved it. ''We went to that awful pizza place, then came back here and went swimming. I used the pool heater, by the way.'' She turned on the oven. ''Then Kathryn Brandt came by and we had a lovely visit.''

''What?'' Clint said sharply. ''Kathryn came by? And stayed, even though I wasn't here? Why?''

''I wondered that myself. But apparently she was at loose ends and just came in for a chat.''

''And what did you two chat about?''

Sensing his annoyance, Regina hesitated. ''Girl stuff. She visited with Katie, had some lemonade, answered some questions for me.''

''Questions about what?'' He sat back down at the counter.

''What you suspect.'' Regina unrolled the biscuits

on a baking sheet and stuck them in the oven. "I wanted to know about your marriage—if you were happy, why you left this lovely house empty for so long."

"I told you why."

"Yes, but I wanted to know more. I like you, Clint, and I'm very interested in both your good and bad times. Unlike you," she added, pouring eggs into a skillet.

Clint reared back. "Now what's that supposed to mean?"

Did you invite Caroline to Nairobi? Don't, she warned herself. *You don't want to go there.* "It means that you aren't too interested in me, in what makes me tick. But then, there's not much there to hold your interest."

"Oh, bull!" he exploded. "I don't know anyone who could hold a candle to you when it comes to valor. You take on the colossal responsibility of a handicapped child and raise her to be the lovely person she is today, you fight for a place in that school she attends, your house burns down—you lose everything...." He took a breath. "And then you move into my house just as nice as you please. That took guts, too. I could have been a bastard instead of the near saint I am."

Regina's laughter blessed his ears. Her hands were free for the moment, so he caught them and kissed each palm. "I'm sorry you thought you weren't interesting. It's just hard for me to get that close. Talking is much more intimate than sex, as I suspect you know."

Regina couldn't answer immediately. His tender gesture had tugged at her heartstrings. "Yes, I do know. I'm surprised that you know, though. Men usually block out personal insights. Too risky. Although I don't know why you guys feel that way."

"Because it makes it easier to control our part of the relationship," he said bluntly. "Verbal intimacy leaves you open for all sorts of problems. Women take those enormous leaps to conclusions that aren't really…real. And believe it or not, most men don't want to hurt their women."

Regina merely nodded. Revealing her feelings would serve no useful purpose and might even turn him off. "I see. Well, I promise not to make any enormous leaps tonight."

From the corner of her eye she saw his mouth move and heard something perilously close to a guffaw. When she looked directly at him, he was gazing across the room, the image of preoccupied innocence.

"So get the biscuits out of the oven and let's eat," she said briskly. "Then we'll play a little poker, get my money back from this card shark I've taken to my bosom."

An eyebrow arched. "Strip poker?"

"If you dare," she said with an insouciant toss of head. It was frightening to be this happy. But she had no control over this emotional roller coaster she rode. All she could do was hold on tight and hope for the best.

After their impromptu dinner, they drove to the park and took a long walk. Lulled by the euphoria of being together, Regina was content to stroll quietly by his side, linking fingers now and then. Her thoughts darted from subject to subject, but always returned to the question that kept popping up when she least expected it. *Where will he be on Thanksgiving Day? And with whom?*

She later took her question to bed with her, where it itched like a burr under the skin. But she did not voice it.

When she lay in his arms listening to his fast heart-beat slowing to normal, she held her tongue. Nodding off to sleep in the sublime warmth radiating from his body to hers put an end to speculation, at least for a little while.

Regina awoke to find herself alone, which didn't startle her anymore. She knew by now that he got restless close to dawn and liked to roam the hushed, gray stillness that preceded sunrise.

Yawning, she gave into a slow, voluptuous stretch. Memories of last night evoked a kitten-and-cream smile. Their lovemaking had been so wonderful, and afterward, so euphoric that she'd felt in danger of melting.

He felt the magic, too—she knew he did! Tender-ness is very hard to fake, she thought drowsily. The way he had kissed her, the possessive embrace, the languid, caressing touch, all bespoke something deeper than affection.

She had called him "beloved" and felt him tense. But her fiery kiss had created a different kind of ten-sion, she recalled with a soft laugh. And when they slept, he held her close. Which made it difficult; she didn't like to sleep close. But she could not bear break-ing free of the heaven of his arms.

Throwing back the covers, she got up to go to the bathroom. When she passed his dresser, she paused, eyeing the clutter of personal belongings. A small pocketknife, change, wallet, keys...and something else that stopped her breath. She hadn't noticed it last night, but even in this dim light she could identify the airline emblem.

Urged on by curiosity, she fought a battle with herself for all of ten seconds before opening the envelope. A round-trip ticket with a dated return to Nairobi.

Sliding the ticket back into its envelope, she replaced it in the same position as she'd found it and grabbed hold of the dresser's beveled edge for support. *Why so shocked, Gina? He told you he was returning to Nairobi, you've never been in the dark about that.*

Regina accepted the mental reprimand; she'd known he would eventually leave. But *eventually* was the key word, she thought. It was loose and open, stretching out to infinity if one chose—instead of running together to form ten measly days.

Slowly she walked on to the bathroom. When she returned to bed, she lay for a time staring at the ceiling, her eyes stinging. "Get a grip, Flynn," she admonished harshly. "That ticket's probably been lying there for weeks—you just didn't notice it before. Been too busy in this room to notice much of anything," she added with a bleak smile.

Recalling the first time she'd made a decision concerning Clint Whitfield gave her mind something else to gnaw on. *That first night, standing over this wonderfully dark, dangerous male while he slept on the couch, pondering her choices; wake him and be through with it, or just let him sleep and ride whatever horse the morning brings.*

Remembering, Regina drew a deep breath. She had made her choice. There was no going back. Morning had come, she reflected, and brought both awesome pleasure, and the possibility of a heartbreak too deep to be borne.

"So ride your horse, Regina, and stop whining about it," she chided her fearful self.

Turning onto her side, she drifted into dreamless slumber, unaware of the man who stood beside her bed, watching her sleep.

Eleven

Monday morning Clint left for San Francisco. He was glad to be going somewhere; a cool front had arrived, both outside and inside his house. He hadn't a clue as to the cause of the chill in the air. In fact, he was nonplussed at even noticing Regina's oh-so-subtle withdrawal. It implied a sensitivity he felt sure he didn't possess. And if he did, as strange as it seemed, then there had been a radical change in his nature.

That made him nervous. A man's character did not change without serious cause. So boarding a plane to San Francisco gave him an absurdly strong sense of relief. Now if he could just turn off his mind....

The visit with his brother went well, although an edge of awkwardness plagued their time together. Tall, slim and fine featured, Brad Whitfield, an attorney, seemed to have little in common with his younger sibling. But he loved San Francisco and took two days off work to show his brother the town.

Clint found himself thinking how romantic this misty, audacious, picture-postcard city would be for lovers. Regina's face came to mind, and there was no turning her off. He thought about her while on delightful little cable cars, aboard the tourist boat plying the harbor and at other points of interest. In his brother's guest bedroom late at night, with the blast of foghorns for a sleeping potion, he couldn't stop thinking of her.

When he left San Francisco Wednesday afternoon, there was affection in the brothers' goodbyes. Clint wondered if they had forged a new bond, and if so, would it last?

Regina's flat declaration rang in his ears. *Family is so important, Clint.* He still didn't agree with that, not wholeheartedly at any rate. He'd gotten out of the habit of being part of any family, and it wasn't that bad, he told himself. Some men were meant to be loners.

Defiantly his mind flew ahead of the plane, to his house in Texas and the woman waiting there. Admittedly he'd missed her. Leaving her again was going to be a bit more difficult than he'd bargained for.

As if to underscore that admission, anticipation bubbled in his veins like fine champagne as he drove home from Houston's busy airport.

Then it all went flat. Regina wasn't there to greet him in her own inimitable way.

The hurt of her absence went deep—too deep. He shoved it far to the back of his mind, burying it with sardonic denial. "Just a dark house to welcome me home," he grumbled, listening to his message machine.

"Tuesday, 10:00 a.m. Clint, I have to go to Dallas for a few days. I'm organizing their new office, so I'm not sure exactly how long I'll be there. See you!''

Clint replayed the message. Then, still grumbling, he went into the kitchen. He was hungry. He'd planned on one of Regina's lovely little suppers she made with such ease. Unfortunately he didn't even know how to boil an egg. He ate cold cereal and told himself he didn't miss her all that much after all.

Liar! scoffed his heart. He ignored it.

She didn't call that night and he didn't have her number. The next night was just as aggravatingly blank. Remembering that he seldom called her on out-of-town trips didn't help. He didn't want to be obliged to call her. He didn't want to care if he did or not. There were so many things here he didn't want, couldn't allow himself to want. And yet he did.

Maybe that's why he felt this keen longing for Africa, he mused. Africa made no emotional demands on him. Africa was *safe*. He needed that now. He felt so edgy, he couldn't sit down because he couldn't stay still that long.

Walking outside to the moonlit deck, he tried picturing his favorite pastimes: standing atop a kopjes, a rocky outcropping that raised his view above the flat plains, watching a pride of lions as playful as kittens, snoozing in the noonday sun.

And he enjoyed being with his Masai friends, tall, proud, elegant men who lived exactly as their ancestors did, yet who had accepted him into their midst. Regina would love to be included in that scene, he thought. *After he introduced her, they would drive to a particularly beautiful place he knew and make love in the tall grass....*

"Oh, hell, Clint," he said with a snort. "Something would come along and either eat her, bite her or burrow into her skin. Which pretty well precludes ever living out that particular fantasy."

Defeated by this strange visceral yearning, he went to bed, only to endure another form of edginess. Clad in pajama bottoms, he paced a path that took him past her bedroom, down the hall to the kitchen where six African violets flaunted their serene beauty and back to his rumpled bed. He could feel the pressure inside him growing, twisting and turning, seeking an outlet. His usual tried-and-true method of containing negative energy had apparently worn thin. He felt explosive.

Friday, the message machine spoke again; she would be home around six. As he replayed her message he felt something akin to a tornado tearing through his emotional center. Gladness, yes. Anticipation, oh, yes. But darker emotions, too. He couldn't name them, but they were there, tangling up his breathing apparatus with their power.

Needing something to calm his nerves, he put on a tape of traditional Kenyan music featuring a deep bass rhythm and clipped, clear-toned guitar patterns. The guitar mimicked the sound and playing technique of the *nyatiti,* an ancient lute. Closing his eyes, he fell into sync with the mesmerizing rhythm…

Despite the music filling the great room, the sound of Regina's little car driving into the garage was as noticeable to him as a herd of stampeding elephants.

"Clint? I'm home!" she announced, coming into the room.

A savage gust of anger thrust words through his lips. "So you are," he said thinly. She wore a red dress, black hose and black pumps, and he was dying to kiss her.

"Yes. That is, I think I am!" she replied with a nervous laugh. Her nose wrinkled. "My goodness, what's that music?"

"*Benga*. It's African."

"Oh. I like it. Kind of makes you want to dance!" Tossing her purse on the counter, she arched an eyebrow. "You don't seem too pleased to see me."

"I'm so bloody pleased to see you, I could take you right here on the floor," he rasped. Desire was eating him alive and he couldn't stand it a second longer. He caught her to him with hands that ached furiously to hold, touch, possess.

Her delectable mouth opened on a surprised little "Oh!" and he kissed it for a long time. Kissed her until he felt only the pure sweetness and beauty of loving her...

When he drew back, her eyes slowly opened, her lips, softly bruised, were a magnet for his mouth. Still kissing her, he reached behind her head to free her hair from imprisoning pins. The unruly curls cascaded down around his hands, his wrists, her neck. He tasted the fragrant spot behind one shell-pink ear. Roaming free, his willful hands slid down her back to the enticing curves of her bottom. There was nothing on her body that was not beautiful, and pleasurable to touch.

"Clint," she murmured, melting into him. "My darling," she whispered on his lips.

For a microsecond he stilled, feeling the endearment as well as hearing it. Sensibly he let its enchantment surge outward and dissipate. Then, ravenous for the joy of mating with her, he steered her to his bedroom.

Somehow his jeans and T-shirt came off; in the

same magical way, the red dress fell in a pool around her feet. The black panty hose were more difficult and he finally had to set her down to remove them. Tossing them over his shoulder, he fell onto the bed with her in his arms.

It was too easy to love her, some dark part of him warned.

Too pleasing to join with her and make that sublime flight to the stars.

Too wonderful to lay here afterward, holding her, drifting down from terrifying heights.

His euphoria abruptly shredded as awareness returned full force. He had given too much. Always before, there was a secret part of himself he kept inviolate, a safe place that no one—*no one*—was allowed to enter. But this woman had breached his armor as easily as taking candy from a baby, he thought, feeling exposed.

Seeking to reassure himself, he gazed down into her upturned face. Her eyes were closed, her smile sweetly content. All those unnerving "wants," both the nameless and the known, surged up so strongly they demanded an immediate response from him. Withdrawing his arm from under Regina's neck, he got out of bed.

"Clint?" she questioned, eyes still closed.

"Shh, it's all right," Clint replied automatically. Standing on one foot and then the other, he pulled on his jeans and left the bedroom.

Regina watched him leave. A sense of wrongness undermined her contentment. She got up and went to the bathroom. Her hair was a witch's broom, she thought, smoothing it as best she could. Still, she had the glow of a woman superbly loved.

"Physically loved," she reminded her tousled image. "Airline ticket, remember?" A quill of sadness came to rest beside the residue of joy. Going to her own room, she slipped a green silk kimono over her nude body. Then, sashing it tightly, she went after Clint.

He stood before the window overlooking the pool, hands crammed in his pockets, shoulders hunched. Low in the background, *Benga* still played.

"Clint, would you…" Regina cleared her throat— there was something alarming about that shutting-out stance. "Are you hungry?"

He wheeled, his eyes suddenly the hot blue color of gas flames. "Yes, I'm hungry!" he exploded. "I damn well don't like it, but there it is, implacable!"

Nerves jumped in her stomach. *Might as well get this over with.* "What don't you like?" she asked, moving to stand beside him.

"Feeling so needy," he ground out. "Feeling this urgency, this hunger, this damned *craving.*"

"Clint, you have to get past that. You have to come to grips with her death," Regina stated. "I know it's hard—"

"I'm talking about you," he grated. "You are driving me flat-out crazy!"

"Oh," Regina whispered, staggered by his admission. She wanted to ask how and why, but doubted she'd like his answers. Still, she had to try. "Maybe what you're feeling is love," she responded softly.

He gave a harsh laugh. "I doubt that. I have to doubt it, because I sure as hell don't want it."

"Why?"

The single word, coupled with the green purity of her gaze, clawed at his heart. "Because I'm too smart to fall for that. Because I know love's tricks. It makes a man hostage to fortune, no matter how good it was. And it was good, Regina. I loved my wife with all my heart and soul.''

''I've already discerned that, Clint. But it's wonderful, isn't it? To love like that—''

''Wonderful? Love isn't sweetness and light, Regina. Love slams you, drives you to stupid acts. And eventually rips your heart out,'' he ended raggedly.

''But isn't it worth it, Clint? You had the profound pleasure of loving someone so much, you feel only half alive when you lose her. That's really rare, Clint. Not many people ever feel that deeply. Most make do with superficial affection, because that's all they'll ever get.''

She touched him. He jerked away. ''You, spouting off like that,'' he raged, ''about something you haven't a clue—it's infuriating! There are things you don't know, things I haven't told another soul.''

''Like what?''

''Like, I was to blame for my wife's death!''

''No, you weren't'' came Regina's swift denial. Standing behind him, she grasped his shoulders. ''Kathryn told me you were carrying a ton of guilt, but truly, your wife's death was not your fault. It was an accident. Put the responsibility where it belongs— on the driver who ran the light!''

He shook his head. ''No, I have to bear part of the blame,'' he ground out, wheeling to face Regina, then back to the window. ''We had a whale of a fight that evening, over this flooring, this damned kitchen *floor!*'' he said, the words pouring out like a river breaching a dam. ''I thought we had settled on a reasonably priced tile, one I could afford. But she went

over my head and had the builder install this costly
Italian stuff. When I walked in here and saw it, I went
ballistic. We'd already gone way over budget on other
things—the roof, the pool…''

He drew in air. ''And then, this floor… We were
still at it when we left for a party. I wanted to drive
my truck. She opted for her little sports car. So I said,
'Fine, you drive us, then. You're in the driver's seat
on everything else. Why stop now?' I can still hear
my ugly, sarcastic tone.''

Clint flinched from Regina's soothing hand. ''Don't
you see? I should have been driving—it should have
been *me* behind that mangled steering wheel!'' he
rasped. ''He hit us broadside, you see. Killed her, left
me relatively untouched. I'll never be able to forgive
myself for…'' He shook his lowered head.

''For living? For going on with your life while hers
ended?''

''Yes, dammit, yes! I should have been the one!''
He dragged in a ragged breath. ''I loved her— God,
I did love her! Losing her tore huge chunks out of my
life—emptiness I can't bear, holes I can't fill…'' His
voice choked off in a guttural sob. And suddenly, all
the tears he hadn't shed, at the hospital, the funeral,
the cemetery, in his cold, empty bed, rushed up
through a break in the wall he'd created so long ago.
Like a blistering geyser, they erupted, pouring through
his throat, his eyes, his nose.

The pain of it bent him double. The noises he made
were appalling—but he couldn't stop. He had no more
control over this unmanly scene than a bereft child.

Regina didn't know what to do. He shook off her
attempt to commiserate with him. Finally, aching to
help, she threw her arms around him and just held on.

Her firm embrace stripped away his last shred of control. Though blazingly embarrassed, desperate to get out of this humiliating situation, he lacked the will to act.

Long seconds passed before he got a grip on himself. Pulling free, he turned his back to her. "I'm sorry," he said, his voice still jagged with effort. "I'm so sorry."

"Nothing to be sorry for, Clint" came her soothing response. "Obviously you still have a lot of stuff to work through."

She hugged him, her body contouring his as she moved in close behind him. "If you're so greedy that you want to take all the blame, then you're not going to like what I have to say. But I'll say it anyway."

"I figured you would," he muttered to Regina.

"Ha." Her embrace tightened. "You have to share the blame, Clint, because you have a right to be hurt and angry. Because it's wrong for one partner to make arbitrary decisions, wrong to change or alter plans without taking into consideration the other partner's opinion."

He didn't respond. She laid her cheek on his back. "Don't be embarrassed about crying, Clint. If more men could do that, there'd be far fewer abused spouses in the world. Getting rid of all that pain and grief you had bottled up inside must have been a wrenching experience. But don't you feel better now?"

Clint's mouth twisted painfully awry. He did feel different—sort of hollow inside, like an empty husk. And so embarrassed it hurt, he completed his quick check of the mess that was Clint Whitfield.

Her arms dropped, letting him turn to face her. He did so with considerable reluctance.

"Nothing has changed, Regina," he said hoarsely. "I still hold myself to blame, and I suspect I always will. So let's drop it, okay?"

Her chin shot up. "No, we're not going to drop it! If you must condemn yourself, then at least remember that there's such a thing as a second chance. And according to God, you deserve it." Then came that wonderfully sweet, impish smile that unhinged him even more. "You going to argue with God, Clint?"

Still snarled in the flood of painfully tangled emotions, Clint laughed through his nose. Feminine foolishness, he thought. He couldn't wait to get out of here.

Regina sobered, her gaze darkening with the courage necessary to continue this risky dialogue. "I love you, Clint. I've loved you since the moment I walked out of the pantry and saw you standing there scowling at me."

He looked dismayed. "Lord, I hope not. Regina, you know I care for you. But caring isn't love. If I've hurt you, I'm so damned sorry. I shouldn't have let things go this far, knowing my heart belongs to another," he said wearily.

Clint stepped back from her, his face a mask again.

But I know the man behind that mask, Regina thought fiercely. *And I know one more thing. I know he loves me.*

Meeting his veiled gaze threw her for a moment. Rallying, she refused to give substance to the doubts ravaging her mind; she would not be second best in his heart. She held out her hands. "Clint—"

"Regina, no." He shook his head against her unspoken plea. "I think I'd better leave, now, before I inflict any further damage on what has to be the sweetest, softest and possibly the most foolish, heart in the world.''

Regina's head lowered. ''Maybe you're right about the foolish part. But I do love you. I think you love me, too. That's why this blowup. Even risking love again must strike you as lunacy. Maybe even a betrayal of what you had with Barbara. But it's not. Truly, it's not, my darling.''

Clint sighed and rubbed his face with a harsh hand. ''I never should have come back here in the first place, should've just turned this house over to a Realtor and stayed where I was, doing something useful with my life...inside of messing up yours.''

''You haven't messed up my life, Clint.'' Her voice picked up urgency. ''Unrequited love has a few perks, you know. One is having the chance to know what the real thing feels like. It's possible that, had we never met, I wouldn't have discovered the glory of true love.''

She gave a short laugh. ''Not that I'm singing hosannas right now. Like you say, love hurts.''

She walked to the kitchen and put on the kettle. ''You want a cup of tea?''

''I want a shot of brandy.'' Striding to the built-in bar, Clint poured two fingers of brandy, then said, ''Oh hell,'' and poured some more. The first sip burned a passage all the way to his toes. It felt wonderful. He swigged the fiery drink, breathing easier as it filled the empty nooks and crannies of his being.

In the kitchen, Regina poured hot water over a green-tea bag. There was a ravening beast loose in her chest, its claws shredding tender, virginal places of the heart. She didn't know how long she could keep up this nerve-racking pretense.

"I saw your airline ticket, so I'm aware of your plans to leave." She spooned sugar into the murky liquid. "That's just a week away. When were you planning to let me in on your plans?"

"I meant to tell you last week, but you went out of town just as I was getting back. So…" He shrugged. The brandy scorched another path down his throat. "You know you're welcome to continue living here. There's no longer any urgency in selling this place."

Her head jerked up. "Thank you, but I'll be moving on, too. Find a nice little house to rent, make Katie a lovely room of her very own. I do appreciate your good-hearted generosity, Clint. Living here these few months has helped me put something aside. So don't go fretting about me. I'll be fine."

Her clear green gaze tangled with his, and won. "I do have one request, though. That you leave tonight. From this house, I mean. I don't think I can stand any more…anymore." Picking up her teacup, she slid a saucer under it. "Good night, Clint. And goodbye, too, I guess. Have a good life, you hear?"

Giving him a lips-only smile, she left him for the much-needed privacy of her own room.

Twelve

Regina awoke Monday morning to gray skies and a dull headache. Silencing her alarm clock, she curled into a comforting ball of limbs and let that last scene with Clint play itself out. Then she sifted through the silence, seeking his presence in the house. All she heard was the air conditioner's hum.

The stillness was smothering her! Bolting from bed, she threw on a robe and hurried to the kitchen. The fragrance of coffee, set to brew at six each morning, gave a lift to her senses. Noting that it had not been touched brought her back down again.

Mocking herself, she ran down the hall to his bedroom. She knew he wouldn't be there, but still she had hope. The door was open, the bed still rumpled.

A quick search of the bathroom pointed out the absence of shaving gear. Viewing his empty closet again was anticlimactic. He was still gone.

"Of course he's gone, Gina," she muttered furiously. "You told him to go. In fact, you practically threw him out—of his own house!"

Regina sank down on his bed, her heart thudding painfully against her rib cage. Where had he gone? He still had four days before his scheduled Kenyan flight. Finding a place to bunk for three days wouldn't be a problem; he had plenty of friends in town. Male and female, she added, thinking of the golden-haired Caroline.

Dropping her face into her hands, Regina battled a forlorn urge to cry. He'd left her! It was still a shock— she'd never really believed he would. Deep down out of logic's reach, she had banked on the magic of their love affair to hold him here.

"Maybe it was just an affair. Nothing special, the common run," she thought aloud. But her heart couldn't accept that; there was nothing common about their lovemaking. At least not for her. But for him? He was so experienced and worldly. Women must chase after him like flocks of hungry pigeons.

"That doesn't mean he takes advantage of all the sexual opportunities open to a man like him," she whispered. "He has far too much integrity for indiscriminate sex."

For a moment her heart questioned, pouring out doubts that had to be conquered one by one. "He'll be back," she told herself, walking out of Clint's bedroom and closing the door behind her. "He just needs time to sort himself out. He'll be back."

Using that litany as a balm for heartache, Regina dressed for the office, her face pale and set. There was always something to occupy her mind. "One day at a time," she advised her dejected image.

* * *

The week passed in a drab succession of uneventful hours. November tenth was etched on her mind in big red letters. When it, too, passed without the call she stupidly anticipated, Regina raged at her enduring hope.

But, oh God, how she ached to hear his voice!

"Or at least some word from him," she fumed, pacing the darkened house, a pale ghost flitting from room to room. She didn't know who to call about his whereabouts, except for his attorney. But she was reluctant to do so. What could she say? *Would you tell him I want him to come home?* Not hardly. This house wasn't home to him.

Or her, either, for that matter, Regina realized as another week crawled by. Decisions had to be made. The most urgent was finding another place to live.

Relaying her decision to her boss was difficult. "If Mr. Whitfield wishes to continue the house-sitter service, I'll see to that," she assured Lamar.

"I should hope so," Lamar muttered, peering at her over his rimless glasses. He had sharp brown eyes, thin brown hair and jowls flowing seamlessly into his neck. "At any rate, you're stuck there until he does express his wishes."

Regina kept her voice neutral as she accepted his implied reprimand. She deserved it.

But Clint hadn't notified her of his wishes either way. "So what else is new?" she muttered furiously, closing his file with a *snap!*

Reining in her anger, she sent him notice of her intent to vacate his house. The only address she had was the one used throughout his absence—his attorney's.

To her astonishment, Lamar received a call from that law firm the very next morning. ''According to Whitfield's attorney,'' Lamar said when she answered his summons, ''you made a verbal contract to remain in the house until it's sold, be that a month from now or six months.''

''But Lamar, a friend of mine has already found me another place to live—''

''I'm sorry, Regina, but you're stuck.''

''A fine little house I can lease with option to buy.'' Regina hurried on. ''It even has a big backyard, oh, and a porch, too! My friend says the offer won't last very long and I really wanted...'' She trailed off as Lamar tented his hands.

''That's tough, but remember, you're the one who set this whole thing in motion,'' he said brusquely.

Regina sighed. ''Yes, I did,'' she agreed with a wan smile. ''Okay, I'm still house-sitting. Thank you, Lamar, for standing behind me. I'm very grateful.''

His response was a throaty grunt. Taking that as a nice way of saying scram, she thanked him again and fled his office.

To her further amazement, a Realtor appeared the next day to assess the house. Clint was moving fast on this, she thought dazedly. She hadn't expected that. She disliked the lockbox on the front door, resented having people wandering through her house—her things, she corrected hastily—when she was at work.

She also hated rising each morning to face the mirror, Regina thought, scowling at her reflection. Puffy, reddened eyes testified to nights spent weeping instead of sleeping.

Sitting at her dressing table, she opened a jar of liquid makeup, her gaze wistful. Regardless of the cost, she could not regret knowing and loving Clint Whitfield. It would be vanity to pretend otherwise. Her need for him was so achingly deep and constant that she would have flown into his arms were it possible.

But he'd have to come to her. Responsibilities prevented her from going to him, mainly her devotion to her young sister. Katie could never make it alone. The sheltered environment of her school wasn't enough; she still needed the security of knowing her big sister was always nearby, watching over her.

"Otherwise I'd be on a plane to Nairobi today," Regina muttered. Gazing into her vulnerable eyes, she made another of her impulsive decisions. Since she couldn't follow him to Africa, she would swallow her pride and send him a verbal message via his attorney.

"Take all the time you need, love. I'm here," the message said. A stupid move on her part? "Well, you've made so many. What's one more?" she asked herself wryly. She peered into the mirror. Thank heavens for makeup. No one would guess by her demeanor that her heart was breaking.

Mid-November was a heady reminder of the vagaries of Texas weather. Bright, balmy days stretched out like a lover's promise, with about as much validity, Clint thought, lifting a pitchfork load of hay over the paddock fence. In Kenya the rains would have begun, bringing to life the wildflowers that starred plains and hills alike with living jewels. The water holes would be filled with life, a fine place for both animal and bird-watching.

But he wasn't anywhere near Kenya. Instead of leaving as scheduled, he'd canceled his flight and driven to West Texas to spend some time with his folks.

Thank God for that impulsive decision, he thought, forking up another load of hay. Three days after he had arrived, his father had undergone a triple bypass. Seeing the man Clint had always considered a tower of strength lying in a hospital bed, fragile and vulnerable, was a visceral blow. Even his mother seemed to have shrunken.

Providing emotional support for his parents was overwhelming at times. But he was immensely grateful for his father's recovery—he couldn't have endured the death of another loved one. Missing Regina was heavy enough.

Responding to a touch on his arm, he turned to face his father, whose walk down to the barn gave substance to the exasperated "I'm fine!" declaration he made at the first hint of concern. The older man had rejected a suggestion to notify his other son about his illness. Clint had honored his wishes, but not happily.

He forked hay; his father propped a foot on the fence. "Do you still think I oughtta call Brad?" he asked abruptly.

Surprised, Clint replied, "Yes, I do. Why? You thinking about doing it?"

"Yeah. I guess nearly dying makes a man rethink things. My heart stopped beating on that operating table, you know."

Clint nodded. "Yes, sir, they told us. You were lucky, Dad, given a second chance, to my way of thinking."

There's such a thing as a second chance. Regina's sweet voice sang through his mind. "Not everyone gets the chance to try again," he countered flatly.

"I don't know about that, Clint. But I guess a man's character is formed without him having much say about it," the older man said in oblique reference to his absent son. When Clint just nodded, he continued, "I thought we might call and invite Brad for Thanksgiving, have a family dinner again. I've got a hunch he'd come. Your mother would be real pleased if he did."

"So call him and ask him."

"Yeah, I will. One other thing, Clint. It concerns the disposal of our property after your mother and I are gone. I figure neither of you boys have any great love for this place, so you won't want to carry on tradition," the elder Whitfield said dryly. "Your ma doesn't, either. She's disliked living here ever since the day I brought her here from Georgia. She'd leave tomorrow if she could. She pines for somewhere with kinder weather."

"Then take her there," Clint said, jolted by his father's loquacity. The old man rarely spoke more than a sentence at a time.

Father glanced at son, his weathered face crinkling with amusement. "Ain't nobody dying to buy us out, Clint. All we have left are the horses and these buildings." He shrugged. "Anyway, here's what I thought. I respect the work you're doing. This place is well watered and there's ample pasturage, so why wouldn't it make a decent animal refuge? I'd will it to you two boys, you pay Brad for his share…"

He trailed off, his keen blue gaze alert for his son's reaction. Which was surprise and confusion, Clint thought, searching for words.

"Dad, if you really want to live somewhere else, I'll buy the ranch for however much you need to get out from under. I can do that now, you know. Money's not a problem. So let's both just think on what all we've said.''

The gray head nodded agreement. ''Oh, I almost forgot, you got a couple messages from your attorney. I wrote 'em down.'' He fumbled in his pocket and unearthed a folded note, handing it to his son.

Clint read it, his face impassive despite the tumult within. One message was from his friend Caroline, stating her decision to holiday in Kenya. The second message was from Regina.

''Nice message,'' his father said, eyeing him.

Of course, he'd written it down. ''Yes sir, very nice.'' Clint pocketed the note. ''Thanks.''

''That second message is just between you and me.''

They shared a smile. ''Thanks again,'' Clint said. *I've got to get off from under this load of emotional hubris,* he mused, watching his father's steady progress back to the house.

Savagely Clint speared another forkful of fodder. When he left Houston, he'd wanted only to forget and slide back into the safety shell of work. Otherwise he'd be needing a padded room, he thought with black humor.

Work had sufficed before. It didn't now. During his time at the ranch, he had plunged into this menial, mind-numbing labor as often as possible, enjoying the burn of overstressed muscles.

That's about all he'd enjoyed, Clint thought. His jaw set, he began mucking out the stalls. He was serious about buying the ranch, and it would be his money, not Barbara's. A few months after he inherited her fortune, he'd taken a big chunk of it and invested in volatile, high-tech stocks. A risky move, but he'd made out like a bandit; enough to repay her trust fund and a bundle for himself. Nothing to brag about, he chided the swift flare of pride. He'd taken a risky gamble and lucked out.

Finishing his chores, he put away his tools and stepped outside. Evening shadows striped the summer-seared pastures. Wearied in both body and spirit, he saddled a horse and set off down a well-worn trail at a fast clip, bent low, riding hard, as if to escape his personal demons.

By the time he returned to the stables, the night was crisp and sparkled with hoarfrost under a full moon. He had hoped the change of scenery would ease some of his inner torment. But his mind still buzzed like a hive of honeybees.

Dismounting, he gave the horse a rubdown and turned her loose. Katie had wanted to ride his horse, he remembered, a smile softening his mouth. Tansy would be a good one for her first time on a horse....

Recalling the experience of finding Katie and then walking back to the house with her hand in his created another kind of ache. She was still very childish in appearance, but how would Regina handle her physical maturity?

"Alone," he muttered, feeling the pang deepen.

Setting a foot on the rail fence, he forced out painful thoughts by focusing on purchasing the ranch from his parents. They could go wherever they wanted; he could pay cash. *Thanks to you, my lovely wife. In my deepest heart I will always cherish your memory. You will never be forgotten.*

The promise felt lighter than usual, untainted by

guilt and bitterness. Its sweetness was an unexpected
balm to his spirit.

So swiftly he caught his breath, his mind shot back
to another disturbing subject. Regina. Even just thinking of her uninhibited response to his loving sent a
quiver of fire deep into his belly. The memory of that
first time in his bed with the enchanting Gina still had
the power to confuse him. Nothing could have pre-
pared him for the shattering ecstasy of their lovemaking.

Yearning shuddered through his long frame. He had
hoped to find surcease in this matter of the heart, too.
But standing here under a star-clotted sky, replaying
her message over and over, he found himself in a vir-
tual anguish of spirit.

But this time it wasn't because of some cruel, con-
trolling fate. The future was in his hands, its direction
determined by the decision *he* made, Clint realized
with piercing self-awareness. He truly enjoyed the ad-
venturesome part of his life. New horizons, new people, always something new to obstruct deeper feelings.

But nothing could block his feelings for Regina
Flynn. To his bewilderment, they surpassed anything
he'd ever felt for a woman.

Three weeks of missing her so much his heart
ached, defined those feelings with stunning clarity.
"Oh, God," he whispered, gripping the rail until the
raw wood stung his callused palms. Despite his resolve, despite all his efforts, asinine and otherwise, he
had fallen in love, then gone beyond love, to a tender,
terrifying place of soul-deep need.

A place where he could cry and be considered no
less of a man. Instead, he was set free.

It's your choice, Clint, his spirit-voice spoke from

subterranean depths. *Take that awesome risk and all that it implies, or play it safe and endure this agony of need and longing for the rest of your life.*

Two days before Thanksgiving, Regina left the office early. Flowering shrubs and mellow sunlight gave a fine imitation of a spring day. Its beauty only exacerbated her heartache.

At least now she had an inkling of what Clint felt, Regina thought. The bitterness of loss, even one that could be reversed by a change of heart, was shockingly painful. More and more she understood what he had gone through. And more and more her anger at being dumped—again—mellowed to tender compassion.

Pulling into the garage, she maneuvered her way through sealed boxes, to the kitchen door and straight back to her bedroom. Brief moments later, she was in the shower, standing under tension-easing hot water.

She had planned on having Thanksgiving in the new house. Her plans being unceremoniously scuttled, she was trying to put a positive spin on celebrating the holiday in this beautiful, but essentially cold house. Cold, she thought aside, because it didn't have the master's touch.

She and Katie would dine on take-out turkey and all the trimmings, she decided. Then a trip to the park and later, a video...

Annoyed by the images derailing her train of thought, Regina leaned forward, bracing herself against the shower's slippery wall. She tried to keep her mind on the present, but it was so blasted difficult!

Caroline's spending Thanksgiving in Nairobi. Kathryn Brandt's words kept circling Regina's mind despite her efforts to block them.

"I will *not* wallow in that stupid, low-self-esteem cliché of another-woman jealousy," Regina fumed. Not that there was any need for jealousy; she wasn't even in the running.

"Because I'm a package deal," she whispered, anguished over the reason he'd walked away. He didn't want to take on a handicapped child. Nothing unusual. Most men backed off when presented with such a responsibility.

"Now you don't know that," she argued with herself. "Such a blanket judgment isn't fair."

Fair or not, it felt good to release some of the gall clogging her throat. Turning off the shower, she toweled roughly, her mind racing. Maybe she'd pick up Katie tonight. She'd planned to do that tomorrow, but the house felt so empty.

"Coward," she muttered, selecting her creamy drawstring pajamas, a fine cotton garment that caressed her weary body like a lover's strokes. After pinning up her hair, she slid her feet into satin scuffs and headed for the kitchen.

The doorbell rang annoyingly. She wasn't dressed for company. Peeking through the slivers of clear glass on the ornate front door panel, she caught her breath in shock, in joy, in wild, careening hope.

In the bargain, she rendered herself unable to think, much less speak.

Clint stood on the steps of his house, hat in hand, strangely breathless, heart thudding absurdly hard. What would she say when she saw him? Better still, what would *he* say when he saw *her?* He had so much to say, so many feelings to put into words, but he tended to go mute just when he needed words the most.

"Don't be surprised if she turns into an icicle when she sees you," he warned his ridiculously shaky self. He was no hero. Just a man entangled in the most profound emotions possible. From love, passion, death, loss, grief, to the shock of renewed passion, confusion, love, denial, realization, humility...

God! How had he done it? How had he traveled this terrifying path? And why was he standing here poised to travel it again? He hadn't forgotten how much pain love carries with it. No guarantees, no certainty. Why would he want to take such a risk again, knowing its destructive power?

The door opened and all his questions were immediately answered. She wore those incredibly sexy pajamas. Unruly red-gold curls spilled around her face, and luminous green eyes gazed up at him.

Clint scrambled for words to ease his awkwardness, something lovely, something romantic. Something a woman would want to hear, even from a man who feared the enormous step of committing himself to her.

"I love you!" he blurted.

"Oh!" she said softly, and walked into his arms and wound her arms around his neck.

Clint shuddered with the onslaught of happiness. God, how could he have forgotten how wonderful she was! How could he forget for even a second that she looked like this, felt like this, that he loved her so much, that she was life itself!

The silken warmth of her, the fragility of her slender body, shook him anew. And then her face raised to his, her lips inviting the kiss he could not have stopped if his life depended on it.

When she drew back and nestled her head on his chest, he could not immediately make sense of what he heard. "Yes, I will," she murmured.

"Will what?" he asked.

"Yes, I will marry you," she said. And then he did something wonderful. He threw back his head and laughed uproariously, from the depths of his heart.

His arms tightened, nigh on to crushing her in his exuberant joy. "Oh. Well, thank you," he said. "That was going to be my next question. Will you marry me? But it's been answered, so let's move on. When?"

"Oh, Clint, I don't know—there are so many issues separating us—"

"As you can see, there's very little separating us," he said huskily, fitting her body to his.

She shook her head, her soft curls caressing his chin. "Physically, I have to agree. But I—I thought your friend Caroline was spending Thanksgiving in Nairobi," she said abruptly.

"I know. I'll have to give her a call," he responded carelessly. "Gina, I didn't go to Kenya. I went to my parents' ranch. That's where I've been the past few weeks. Working and brooding. God, I missed you! So, how about today?"

"What? You mean get married today?" she asked incredulously.

"Yep! We'll fly to Vegas, get hitched in one of those little gingerbread chapels, honeymoon in one of their fancy hotel suites for the night—"

"Wait a minute, wait a minute! What about Katie?"

Regina asked breathlessly. "She does have to be factored in, Clint, to whatever we do."

"Let me finish, please?" Clint said sternly. "Tomorrow we'll fly back here—I've rented a plane—pick up Katie and fly to the ranch, have Thanksgiving dinner with my family. Lord, is Mom gonna be surprised!" he exulted. "But not Dad. He read your message."

"Oh! I didn't realize... Clint, there are so many things to work out. That bit about you can't stay and I can't go still holds true, I guess. For my part, upon serious reflection," she said with a spark of humor, "I think I might be a little obsessive about Katie's welfare. She's in a secure setting, with fine, dedicated caretakers, so I don't see why I couldn't take two or three weeks to travel with you—as long as we maintain telephone contact, of course. Oh, Clint, I'd like so much seeing your beloved Serengeti!" She sighed. "But in hard fact, I am still stuck here. While you... I just don't know how that could be worked out. If it could."

"It could work out, it *will,* because we'll make it work out." His voice picked up urgency. "There are so many new avenues opening up for me, Gina! With my exotic-animal experience, I can act as a consultant to zoos, I can reopen my vet clinic. There's Dad's ranch, which I'm buying just so they can get out from under. And as for Katie, between us we can make sure she has a rich, full life."

Clint tipped up her chin. "So, how does my Vegas plan sound? Unless you want a big wedding?"

"No, I don't really care for all the fuss. But I have to be honest, Clint. I love you and I want to be your wife, but not your second... Oh, fiddle, that didn't come out right," she muttered, head back on his chest.

"Regina, I have been blessed to have known real love twice in my lifetime," he said huskily. "It astounds me, really. Why me? Why have I been so lucky? But to answer your question, I love you so deeply, so passionately and tenderly and ardently, that no other woman could ever take your place. You could never be second to anyone, my beloved Gina."

"Thank you, Clint, for understanding," she said, her words muffled by his chest. "I think your plan is wonderful. One thing, though," she added as his hands began intimately roaming.

"What's that?"

"The honeymoon," she said sternly, "comes *after* the wedding."

* * * * *

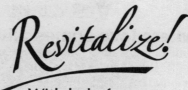

Feel like a star with Silhouette.

We will fly you and a guest to New York City for an exciting weekend stay at a glamorous 5-star hotel. Experience a refreshing day at one of New York's trendiest spas and have your photo taken by a professional. Plus, receive $1,000 U.S. spending money!

**Flowers...long walks...dinner for two...
how does Silhouette Books
make romance come alive for you?**

Send us a script, with 500 words or less, along with visuals (only drawings, magazine cutouts or photographs or combination thereof). Show us how Silhouette Makes Your Love Come Alive. Be creative and have fun. No purchase necessary. All entries must be clearly marked with your name, address and telephone number. All entries will become property of Silhouette and are not returnable. **Contest closes September 28, 2001.**

Please send your entry to: **Silhouette Makes You a Star!**

In U.S.A.	In Canada
P.O. Box 9069	P.O. Box 637
Buffalo, NY, 14269-9069	Fort Erie, ON, L2A 5X3

Look for contest details on the next page, by visiting www.eHarlequin.com or request a copy by sending a self-addressed envelope to the applicable address above. Contest open to Canadian and U.S. residents who are 18 or over. Void where prohibited.

Our lucky winner's photo will appear in a Silhouette ad. Join the fun!

SRMYAS1

HARLEQUIN "SILHOUETTE MAKES YOU A STAR!" CONTEST 1308
OFFICIAL RULES
NO PURCHASE NECESSARY TO ENTER

1. To enter, follow directions published in the offer to which you are responding. Contest begins June 1, 2001, and ends on September 28, 2001. Entries must be postmarked by September 28, 2001, and received by October 5, 2001. Enter by hand-printing (or typing) on an 8 ½" x 11" piece of paper your name, address (including zip code), contest number/name and attaching a script containing 500 words or less, along with drawings, photographs or magazine cutouts, or combinations thereof (i.e., collage) on no larger than 9" x 12" piece of paper, describing how the Silhouette books make romance come alive for you. Mail via first-class mail to: Harlequin "Silhouette Makes You a Star" Contest 1308, (in the U.S.) P.O. Box 9069, Buffalo, NY 14269-9069, (in Canada) P.O. Box 637, Fort Erie, Ontario, Canada L2A 5X3. Limit one entry per person, household or organization.

2. Contests will be judged by a panel of members of the Harlequin editorial, marketing and public relations staff. Fifty percent of criteria will be judged against script and fifty percent will be judged against drawing, photographs and/or magazine cutouts. Judging criteria will be based on the following:

   - Sincerity—25%
   - Originality and Creativity—50%
   - Emotionally Compelling—25%

   In the event of a tie, duplicate prizes will be awarded. Decisions of the judges are final.

3. All entries become the property of Torstar Corp. and may be used for future promotional purposes. Entries will not be returned. No responsibility is assumed for lost, late, illegible, incomplete, inaccurate, nondelivered or misdirected mail.

4. Contest open only to residents of the U.S. (except Puerto Rico) and Canada who are 18 years of age or older, and is void wherever prohibited by law; all applicable laws and regulations apply. Any litigation within the Province of Quebec respecting the conduct or organization of a publicity contest may be submitted to the Régie des alcools, des courses et des jeux for a ruling. Any litigation respecting the awarding of a prize may be submitted to the Régie des alcools, des courses et des jeux only for the purpose of helping the parties reach a settlement. Employees and immediate family members of Torstar Corp. and D. L. Blair, Inc., their affiliates, subsidiaries and all other agencies, entities and persons connected with the use, marketing or conduct of this contest are not eligible to enter. Taxes on prizes are the sole responsibility of the winner. Acceptance of any prize offered constitutes permission to use winner's name, photograph or other likeness for the purposes of advertising, trade and promotion on behalf of Torstar Corp., its affiliates and subsidiaries without further compensation to the winner, unless prohibited by law.

5. Winner will be determined no later than November 30, 2001, and will be notified by mail. Winner will be required to sign and return an Affidavit of Eligibility/Release of Liability/Publicity Release form within 15 days after winner notification. Noncompliance within that time period may result in disqualification and an alternative winner may be selected. All travelers must execute a Release of Liability prior to ticketing and must possess required travel documents (e.g., passport, photo ID) where applicable. Trip must be booked by December 31, 2001, and completed within one year of notification. No substitution of prize permitted by winner. Torstar Corp. and D. L. Blair, Inc., their parents, affiliates and subsidiaries are not responsible for errors in printing of contest, entries and/or game pieces. In the event of printing or other errors that may result in unintended prize values or duplication of prizes, all affected game pieces or entries shall be null and void. **Purchase or acceptance of a product offer does not improve your chances of winning.**

6. Prizes: (1) Grand Prize—A 2-night/3-day trip for two (2) to New York City, including round-trip coach air transportation nearest winner's home and hotel accommodations (double occupancy) at The Plaza Hotel, a glamorous afternoon makeover at a trendy New York spa, $1,000 in U.S. spending money and an opportunity to have a professional photo taken and appear in a Silhouette advertisement (approximate retail value: $7,000). (10) Ten Runner-Up Prizes of gift packages (retail value $50 ea.). Prizes consist of only those items listed as part of the prize. Limit one prize per person. Prize is valued in U.S. currency.

7. For the name of the winner (available after December 31, 2001) send a self-addressed, stamped envelope to: Harlequin "Silhouette Makes You a Star!" Contest 1197 Winners, P.O. Box 4200 Blair, NE 68009-4200 or you may access the www.eHarlequin.com Web site through February 28, 2002.

Contest sponsored by Torstar Corp., P.O Box 9042, Buffalo, NY 14269-9042.

SRMYAS2

COMING NEXT MONTH

#1387 THE MILLIONAIRE COMES HOME—Mary Lynn Baxter
Man of the Month
Millionaire Denton Hardesty returned to his hometown only to find himself
face-to-face with Grace Simmons—the lover he'd never forgotten. Spending
time at Grace's bed-and-breakfast, Denton realized he wanted to rekindle the
romance he'd broken off years ago. Now all he had to do was convince Grace
that *this* time he intended to stay...forever.

#1388 COMANCHE VOW—Sheri WhiteFeather
In keeping with the old Comanche ways, Nick Bluestone promised to marry
his brother's widow, Elaina Myers-Bluestone, and help raise her daughter.
Love wasn't supposed to be part of the bargain, but Nick couldn't deny the
passion he found in Elaina's embrace. Could Nick risk his heart and claim
Elaina as his wife...*in every way?*

#1389 WHEN JAYNE MET ERIK—Elizabeth Bevarly
20 Amber Court
That's me, bride-on-demand Jayne Pembroke, about to get hitched to the
one and only drop-dead gorgeous Erik Randolph. The proposal was simple
enough—one year together and we'd both get what we wanted. But one taste
of those spine-tingling kisses and I was willing to bet things were going to get a
whole lot more complicated!

#1390 FORTUNE'S SECRET DAUGHTER—Barbara McCauley
Fortunes of Texas: The Lost Heirs
When store owner Holly Douglas rescued injured bush pilot Guy Blackwolf
after his plane crashed into a lake by her home, she found herself irresistibly
attracted to the charming rogue and his magnetic kisses. But would she be able
to entrust her heart to Guy once she learned the secret he had kept from her?

#1391 SLEEPING WITH THE SULTAN—Alexandra Sellers
Sons of the Desert: The Sultans
When powerful and attractive Sheikh Ashraf abducted actress Dana Morningstar
aboard his luxury yacht, he claimed that he was desperately in love with her and
wanted the chance to gain her love in return. Dana knew she shouldn't trust
Ashraf—but could she resist his passionate kisses and tender seduction?

#1392 THE BRIDAL ARRANGEMENT—Cindy Gerard
Lee Savage had promised to marry and take care of Ellie Shiloh in accordance
with her father's wishes. Lee soon became determined to show his innocent
young bride the world she had always been protected from. But he hadn't
counted on Ellie's strength and courage to show him a thing or two...about
matters of the heart.

SDCNM0801